U0033923

英語力 2

16堂流利英語聽說訓練課

Listening and Speaking in Everyday Life

作者 Owain Mckimm　譯者 丁宥榆
審訂 Treva Adams

MP3

寂天雲 APP

如何下載 MP3 音檔

❶ 寂天雲 APP 聆聽：掃描書上 QR Code 下載「寂天雲－英日語學習隨身聽」APP。加入會員後，用 APP 內建掃描器再次掃描書上 QR Code，即可使用 APP 聆聽音檔。

❷ 官網下載音檔：請上「寂天閱讀網」（www.icosmos.com.tw），註冊會員／登入後，搜尋本書，進入本書頁面，點選「MP3 下載」下載音檔，存於電腦等其他播放器聆聽使用。

CONTENTS MAP

LISTENING	GRAMMAR	SPEAKING	PRONUNCIATION
◆ 判斷歷史人物的身分 ◆ 聆聽人物描述週末活動 ◆ 聆聽人物的兒時回憶和經驗	◆ 簡單過去式： 　規則和不規則動詞	◆ 描述假期 ◆ 進行關於歷史人物的問答 ◆ 說明不在家的原因	◆ ed 結尾的動詞： 　[t] [d] [ɪd]
◆ 聆聽人物的好惡 ◆ 辨識人物的喜好 ◆ 辨識人物最愛和最恨的事物	◆ like 和 enjoy 的差別	◆ 談論食物和服裝 ◆ 詢問他人最喜愛什麼事物 ◆ 將自己的好惡和全班同學作比較	◆ 擦音： 　[f] [v]；[s] [z]
◆ 聆聽人物未來的計畫 ◆ 填寫月計畫表 ◆ 聆聽朋友討論要買的禮物	◆ 簡單未來式 　（will 和 be going to）	◆ 談論節日計畫 ◆ 邀請某人參加一場活動 ◆ 進行關於未來的問答	◆ 擦音： 　[θ] [ð]； 　[ʃ] [ʒ]；[h]
◆ 在一般對話中進行比較 ◆ 比較人物 ◆ 比較兩樣事物之後作決定	◆ 構成形容詞比較級和最高級的句子	◆ 比較不同國家 ◆ 用比較的方式來售貨 ◆ 誇耀自己的能力或外貌	◆ 阻音： 　[p] [b]；[t] [d]
◆ 辨識人際關係 ◆ 辨識人物談論彼此的方式 ◆ 描述一位朋友	◆ 副詞和形容詞	◆ 推薦朋友 ◆ 談論共同的朋友 ◆ 描述共同的朋友 ◆ 閒聊共同朋友的八卦	◆ 阻音： 　[k] [g]；[tʃ] [dʒ]
◆ 在超級市場遇到的問題 ◆ 尋找喜愛的物品並付款 ◆ 討論價錢	◆ 連接詞 　（and、but、or、 　so、for、yet、nor）	◆ 找到自己想要的物品 ◆ 尋找替代品 ◆ 討價還價	◆ 鼻音： 　[m] [n] [ŋ]
◆ 聆聽緊急通話 ◆ 辨識各種緊急事件 ◆ 應對各種緊急事件	◆ 感官動詞與連綴動詞	◆ 通報緊急事故 ◆ 提供相關資訊給急救單位 ◆ 用不同的方式應對各種緊急事件	◆ 邊音與滑音： 　[l] [j] [w] [r]
◆ 辨識來電者 ◆ 辨識來電原因 ◆ 辨識電話中提到的重要訊息	◆ 不定詞與動名詞	◆ 在電話中針對一般主題進行對談 ◆ 和各種人講電話	◆ 母音（長母音與短母音）： 　[i] [ɪ]

CONTENTS MAP

LISTENING	GRAMMAR	SPEAKING	PRONUNCIATION
◆ 請求協助 ◆ 判斷某人是否有提供協助的意願	◆ 助動詞	◆ 提出和回應要求 ◆ 索取更多某物	◆ 母音（長母音與短母音）： [e] [ɛ]
◆ 從症狀辨識疾病 ◆ 向醫生或老闆描述你的疾病 ◆ 找出適當的疾病治療方式	◆ 助動詞 （do、does、did）	◆ 告訴醫生你的疾病 ◆ 打電話請病假 ◆ 詢問和建議如何改善病況	◆ 母音： [æ] [ɑ]
◆ 談論運動習慣 ◆ 談論不為人知的專長 ◆ 辨識人物從事壞習慣的頻率	◆ 不定代名詞 （one、both、some、most、all…of）	◆ 將你的運動能力和例行運動時間告訴某人 ◆ 談論不為人知的專長 ◆ 說出某人的壞習慣	◆ 母音（長母音與短母音）： [o] [ɔ]
◆ 記錄公寓特徵 ◆ 判斷哪一間公寓最合適 ◆ 辨識室友行為問題並且制訂居家規則	◆ 不定代名詞 （many、much、a few、a little…of）	◆ 進行關於公寓的問答 ◆ 制訂適合雙方的居家規則	◆ 母音（長母音與短母音）： [u] [ʊ]
◆ 叫計程車與付費 ◆ 購買火車票 ◆ 運用旅遊資訊來解決問題	◆ 主動和被動語態 （使用情態助動詞）	◆ 叫計程車與付費 ◆ 在車站購買各種票券	◆ 母音（重母音與輕母音）： [ʌ] [ə]
◆ 描述工時、薪資和福利 ◆ 依據工作描述來辨識人物 ◆ 填寫人力仲介的表格	◆ 附加問句	◆ 進行關於工作的問答 ◆ 表達喜歡和不喜歡工作的哪些方面 ◆ 依據期望的工作內容建議適當的工作	◆ 母音（重母音與輕母音）： [ɝ] [ɚ]
◆ 參觀景點和品嚐新食物 ◆ 描述各種旅遊經驗 ◆ 聆聽旅行全程的描述	◆ 特殊動詞 （stop、try、remember、forget）	◆ 描述假日去處的各種特色 ◆ 談論你所做或經歷的事 ◆ 談論旅行中的住宿	◆ 雙母音： [aɪ] [aʊ] [ɔɪ]
◆ 辦理報到手續和劃位 ◆ 辨識登機證上面的資訊 ◆ 聆聽登機廣播	◆ too…to 和 so…that	◆ 機場報到 ◆ 進海關的問答	◆ 音調簡介

學習及教學導覽

《英語力》是一本訓練英語聽力與口說能力的用書，旨在引領學生認識基礎英語會話。本書練習的編寫，皆是針對與母語人士對談時必備的英語會話，以期協助學生建立信心與理解力。

《英語力》如何協助您增進英文能力？

- 《英語力》提供了與**真實生活相符的情境和對話**，讓您與母語人士日常互動時能泰然自若。

- 本書運用生動而清楚的圖片，輔助您輕鬆學會大量的實用生字。

- 本書用**清楚而簡潔**的方式呈現文法要項，並提供豐富的範例。

- 大量的口語文法練習，讓您在真實生活會話中能正確傳達訊息、避免誤解。

- 針對文意主旨、相關細節和其他具體資訊所設計的**聽力練習**，能訓練您不僅聽懂對話的梗概，也能理解更多前後文所蘊含的意義。

- 針對**關鍵片語**和內文細節所設計的聽力練習，能增進您對英文的了解，更進一步學習進階英語。

- 藉著與主題相關的各種口語練習，您將能熟練運用在本書單字、聽力、文法單元所學到的英文。

- 易懂易學的**會話範例**和輔助學習的會話句型，讓您能不費吹灰之力地自由運用在對話中。

- 透過本書大量的**兩人活動**和小組練習，您能獲得充分的口語實戰經驗。

- **豐富的圖片**和**建議主題**，讓您不再為了找話題而傷腦筋。

- 完善的**發音教學**單元能協助您熟悉英語的基礎發音，提供大量練習各種發音的機會，讓您的發音更像母語人士。

《英語力》是如何編排的？

- 《英語力》有 16 個單元。

- 每個單元分為六個部分。

單元結構：

I. Topic Preview 主題預覽
透過幾則簡短的會話範例，帶您進入主題。

II. Vocabulary and Phrases 字彙和片語
提供相關的字彙和片語，是您有效聽、說的重要工具。

III. Now, Time to Listen! 聽力時間！
透過各種對話、獨白和聽力練習，訓練您的聽力技巧。

IV. Now, Grammar Time! 文法時間！
正式介紹前三部分所應用的文法，並提供練習的機會。

V. Now, Time to Speak! 口語時間！
針對各單元主題，運用小組或兩人練習的方式，提供口說的練習活動。

VI. Now, Time to Pronounce! 發音時間！
每次介紹幾種發音，並提供練習讓您能認識並正確發音。

如何使用《英語力》進行教學？

- 請於每個單元的一開始，先進行 **Topic Preview** 的部分，依照**會話範例進行練習**，讓學生熟悉相關情境。同時利用這一小節來引導與主題相關的一些概念，並評估哪些概念可能較有難度。

- **介紹該單元的生字**，接著進行 **Sentence Patterns** 的教學。讓學生將學到的生字套用在句型裡，以期同時熟悉生字和句型。

- 在進行每一則聽力練習之前，先請學生**預測可能會聽到哪些生字和片語**，讓學生在練習聽力之前先有概念。

- 完成聽力練習之後，鼓勵學生挑選其中一段或數段，**再仔細聽一次，並盡量記住內容**，然後和同學一起練習會話。這是練習口語能力的好機會，也有助於他們記住常用的句型和會話模式。

- 在聽力的小節已經接觸到一些文法之後，學生對於如何使用該單元的文法結構應該已經有了粗略的概念，此時請他們**朗讀例句**，並且試著**造出自己的句子**。記得不時提問相關的問題，以確認學生是否完全理解。

- 本書的許多文法練習是必須兩兩分組進行的口語練習，為了鼓勵學生開口，在他們對話時先不要急著糾正，可以先將您所聽到的錯誤寫下來，在練習進行了幾分鐘之後才暫停，然後全班一起檢討剛才所犯的錯誤，逐一釐清學生不懂的地方。之後再練習一次，確認學生這次用對了文法。

- 本系列套書的口語練習部分，是希望藉由提供學生**大量的句型和輔助資訊**，讓他們盡量在無壓力的情況下開口說英文。如果您認為學生們已經可以自由練習了，就鼓勵他們以 Topic Preview 或者書裡任何一張圖片的情境為基礎，自由發揮對話。

- 在**發音練習**這一小節裡，讓學生先聽一次課本MP3朗讀發音，接著再聽一次，並且跟著播音員覆誦。當您認為學生們練習的差不多了，可以個別點幾個學生測試發音。

- 鼓勵學生盡量自然地**唸出單字的發音**，無須過度強調或加重某個特定的音。

ENJOY learning!
EMPLOY new language!
EMPOWER your English!

享受學習趣！
使用新語言！
活化英語力！

Talking About the Past 談論過去

I. Topic Preview 🎧 001

1 Talking about yourself when you were little 談論你小時候的事

This is me when I was a baby.

You were so cute.

Look! I had blond hair back then.

2 Talking about childhood experiences 談論兒時經驗

I went to Disneyland when I was seven.

When I was seven, I learned how to swim.

3 Talking about history 談論歷史

This is Henry VIII.

Who was he?

15½P
HENRY VIII/MARY ROSE

He was King of England.

When was he king?

He was king from 1509 to 1547.

4 Talking about your vacation 談論度假

Where did you go on your vacation? Did you do anything fun?

I went to Malaysia. I rode an elephant!

5 Talking about your weekend 談論週末活動

What did you do on Saturday night?

I just stayed home and watched a movie.

On Sunday I played soccer with my friends.

I made dinner for my boyfriend.

II. Vocabulary & Phrases

writer
作家

actor
演員

leader / politician
領袖／政治家

musician
音樂家

philosopher
哲學家

queen   king
皇后   國王

athlete
運動員

soldier / warrior
士兵／戰士

artist
藝術家

scientist
科學家

go bungee jumping
去玩高空彈跳

go sightseeing
去觀光

sunbathe
做日光浴

go diving
去潛水

buy souvenirs
買紀念品

Sentence Patterns

Some expressions that you can use when talking about the past:
談論過去的用語：

- I stayed at home and watched TV *yesterday/last night/last week*.
- I went to Malaysia *last summer/two weeks ago/five years ago/ten years ago*.
- He lived *over 100 years ago/2,000 years ago*.
- I learned how to swim when I was *four/seven/ten*.
- I graduated in *2007/1975*.

III. Now, Time to Listen!

Look at the four famous people below. Do you know who they are? If not, ask your teacher. When you know who they are, complete Exercise 1.

| William Shakespeare 莎士比亞 | Abraham Lincoln 林肯 | Confucius 孔子 | Michael Jackson 麥可・傑克森 |

1 Peter and Janet are playing a guessing game. Listen to their conversation and guess the person they're describing. Write the person's name in the space given.

(004)

1 *Person A*   2 *Person B*   3 *Person C*

_____   _____   _____

2 Listen to Angela and Paul talk about their weekend. Then check ☑ the correct box.

(005)

A

1 Paul bought . . .

a ☐   b ☐   c ☐

2 Paul spent . . .

a **50** ☐   b **200** ☐   c **300** ☐

006 Now, listen to the second part of the dialogue.

B

3 On Saturday, Angela went to a . . .

☐   ☐   ☐

4 Angela met Dan, who is a/an . . .

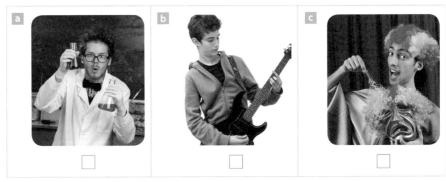

☐   ☐   ☐

5 Angela and Dan did NOT talk about . . .

☐   ☐   ☐

3 Listen to the following people talk about their childhoods. Then match the names to the correct pictures and time expressions. The first one has been done for you.
007

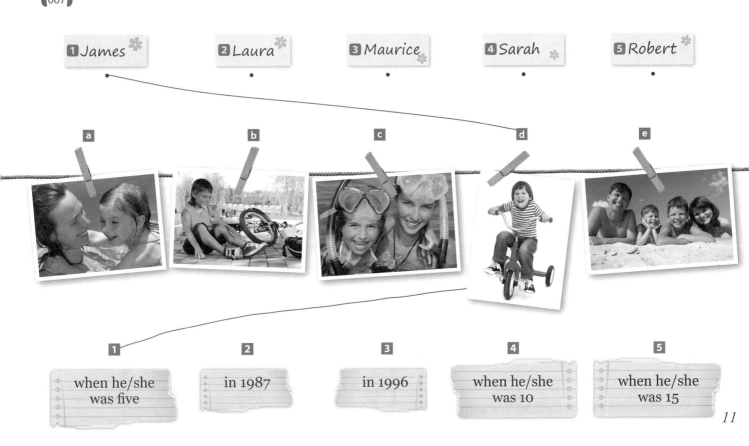

1 James   2 Laura   3 Maurice   4 Sarah   5 Robert

a   b   c   d   e

1 when he/she was five   2 in 1987   3 in 1996   4 when he/she was 10   5 when he/she was 15

IV. Now, Grammar Time!

The Simple Past Tense
Regular and Irregular Verbs
簡單過去式：規則和不規則動詞

	"Be" Verb be 動詞	Regular Verbs 規則動詞	Irregular Verbs 不規則動詞
Affirmative Statements 肯定句	I was thin when I was a child. You were a very happy baby.	I watched TV last night.	I went sightseeing in Paris last year. *(go)*
Negative Statements 否定句	She wasn't a musician. (She was a writer.)	He didn't study English at school.	He didn't read any books last month.
Yes/No Questions 是非問句	Was it sunny in England last week? *Yes, it was. / No, it wasn't.*	Did it rain last Monday? *Yes, it did. / No, it didn't.*	Did we beat the Korean basketball team? *Yes, we did. / No, we didn't.*
WH-Questions WH 問句	Why were they late to the party? *They missed the bus.*	When did they arrive at the restaurant? *They arrived at 7 o'clock.*	Who did you speak to on the phone last night? *I spoke to Jim.*

❹ Write the simple past forms of the following regular and irregular verbs. You may need to check a dictionary for the correct spellings.

Regular Verbs 規則動詞 :
Rules for Verb Endings 字尾變化規則

walk	+ed	walk**ed**
stud**y**	y+ied	stud**ied**
play	+ed	play**ed**
lie	+d	lie**d**
stop	+_ed	stop**ped**

Regular Verbs
★ ★ ★ ★ ★ ★ ★ ★ ★ ★ ★

1 jump _____

2 clean _____

3 hike _____

4 sunbathe _____

5 visit _____

6 rest _____

Irregular Verbs
★ ★ ★ ★ ★ ★ ★ ★ ★ ★ ★

1 buy _____

2 go _____

3 drink _____

4 see _____

5 meet _____

6 swim _____

5 Look at Drew and Lena's holiday photos. Write what they did on each day. You can use some of the verbs from Exercise 4 to help you. The first sentence has been completed for you.

Day 1

drink cocktails

Day 2

go hiking

Day 3

go diving in the ocean

Day 4

go shopping

Day 5

rest on the beach

1 On day one, _Lena and Drew drank cocktails._

2 On day two, _____.

3 On day three, _____.

4 On day four, _____.

5 On day five, _____.

V. Now, Time to Speak!

6 Pair Work! Imagine you went on an amazing vacation last summer. Write what you did each day in the chart. Then tell your classmate about what you did.

Day 1	Day 2	Day 3	Day 4	Day 5
I went . . .	I had / ate . . .			

7 Choose a famous person from history who you know something about. Your classmate (008) must try to guess who he/she is in fewer than 10 questions. Use WH-QUESTIONS and YES/NO QUESTIONS.

First, listen and practice the dialogue as an example.

A	OK. I'm ready.
B	First question: Was this person a man?
A	Yes, he was.
B	Did he play sports?
A	No, he didn't.
B	OK. What did he do?
A	He was an artist, but he also invented many things.
B	Hmm. Did he come from Italy?
A	Yes, he did.
B	Did he paint the *Mona Lisa*?
A	Yes, he did.
B	Is it Leonardo da Vinci?
A	Yes, it is!

8 Listen to the dialogue and practice it with your partner.

(009)	Mike	Where did you go last night?
	Tina	I went to a friend's birthday party. Why?
	Mike	I called your house, but you weren't home. Was it fun?
	Tina	Yes, it was great. Did you do anything exciting last night?
	Mike	Not really. I just made dinner and read a book.

a concert 演唱會

Now, role-play with your classmate.

A	Where did you go _____?
B	I went to _____. Why?
A	I called your house, but you weren't home. Was it fun?
B	Yes/No, it was _____. Did you do anything exciting _____?
A	Not really. / Yeah. I _____.

an amusement park
遊樂園

a movie 電影

VI. Now, Time to Pronounce!

Verbs Ending With "ed" 字尾加 ed 的動詞 [d] [t] [ɪd]

9 Listen and repeat these past tense verbs.

(010)

[d] tried   glued   called   lied   cried   played

[t] liked   hoped   laughed   asked   coached   dressed

(011) Listen and **circle** the words with the [**d**] sound.

1 allowed   **2** washed   **3** begged   **4** buried   **5** jumped   **6** cooked

(012) Now, listen and **circle** the words with the [**t**] sound.

1 braked   **2** beamed   **3** chewed   **4** confused   **5** watched   **6** forced

10 Some past tense verbs have an extra syllable. This is pronounced [ɪd]. Listen and repeat.

(013)

[ɪd] wanted   faded   dusted   alerted   avoided   melted

11 Listen to the words. Then write the correct phonetic symbol—[t], [d], or [ɪd]—

(014) underneath each word.

1 attached	**2** managed	**3** amended	**4** licked	**5** killed
[t]	_____	_____	_____	_____
6 ended	**7** amused	**8** argued	**9** added	**10** missed
_____	_____	_____	_____	_____

I. Topic Preview (015)

1 Discussing food in a restaurant 討論某間餐廳的食物

I love this fish. How's your beef?

It's perfect.

2 Expressing dislike 表達厭惡

I'm not too keen on this salad.

I don't like these vegetables at all.

3 Asking someone's opinion about clothes 詢問某人對於服裝的意見

What do you think of this coat?

I like the style, but I don't like the color.

4 Talking about subjects at school 談論學校科目

Math class is the worst! I really hate it.

I don't like math either, but I love history.

Science is my favorite class.

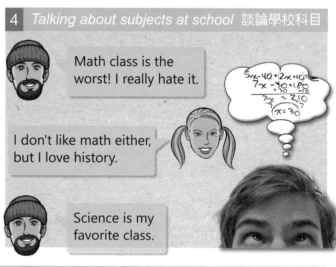

5 Discussing movies 討論電影

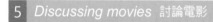

Do you like horror movies?

No. Horror movies are the worst!

Action movies are my favorite.

I'm not a big fan of action movies.

16

II. Vocabulary & Phrases

beef 牛肉

vegetables 蔬菜

pasta 義大利麵

donuts 甜甜圈

seafood 海鮮

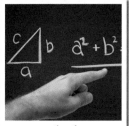
math class
數學課

gym class
體育課

art class
美術課

science class
自然科學課

English class
英文課

horror movies
恐怖片

comedies
喜劇片

sci-fi movies
科幻片

action movies
動作片

romantic movies
愛情片

Sentence Patterns

- I like *seafood*.
  I love *art class*.
  I hate *romantic movies*.
- I don't like *vegetables*.
  I'm not too keen on *math class*.
  I'm not a fan of *comedies*.
  I can't stand *gym class*.
- *English (class)* is amazing!
  Sci-fi movies are the worst.
  Seafood is OK.

- My favorite *kind of movie* is *action movies*.
  My favorite *classes* are *science class* and *math class*.
  Beef is my favorite *food*.
  Sci-fi movies are my favorite *kind of movie*.
  Math and *English* are my favorite *classes*.
- I prefer *horror movies* (to *action movies*).

III. Now, Time to Listen!

1 Listen to Mark and Jane talk about going to see a movie. Then check ☑ True or False.

(018)

True	False	
_____	_____	**1** Jane hates horror movies.
_____	_____	**2** Mark likes comedies.
_____	_____	**3** Jane prefers comedies to horror movies.
_____	_____	**4** Mark doesn't like horror movies.
_____	_____	**5** Jane thinks comedies are OK.

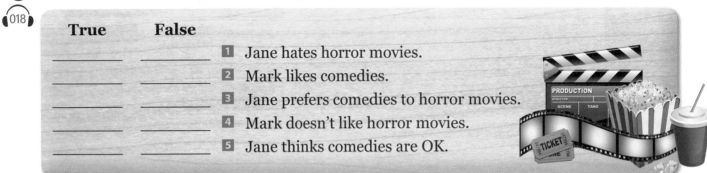

2 Listen to Peter talk about school. Then write "likes," "dislikes," "favorite," or "worst" under each picture.

(019)

1

a _____ b _____ c _____ d _____

2

a _____ b _____ c _____ d _____

3 Listen to the following people express their likes and dislikes. Then match each name to the best description of the speaker.

(020)

1	Dan	•	• **a**	likes to be scared but isn't keen on action movies.
2	Wanda	•	• **b**	hates bright colors but loves to wear black.
3	John	•	• **c**	doesn't like romantic movies but loves comedies.
4	Jenny	•	• **d**	can't stand people who wear only black.
5	Kate	•	• **e**	loves gym class but can't stand math.

IV. Now, Grammar Time!

The difference between "like" and "enjoy"
like 和 enjoy 的不同

Like 喜歡		Enjoy 享受	
I think _____ is/are interesting/fun/great/delicious . . .		_____ give(s) me pleasure / make(s) me feel good.	
like + gerund like + 動名詞	• I like watching movies. • I like swimming. • I like shopping.	enjoy + gerund enjoy + 動名詞	• I enjoy climbing mountains. • I enjoy listening to music. • I enjoy hanging out with friends.
like + to-infinitive like + 不定詞	• I like to travel. • I like to eat seafood. • I like to play basketball.		x
like + noun like + 名詞	• I like science. • I like rock music. • I like this steak.	enjoy + noun enjoy + 名詞	• I enjoy art class. • I enjoy school. • I enjoy baseball.

4 Look at the pictures and finish the sentences using the prompts given. The first sentence has been completed for you.

The girls _like eating pizza._
(like + gerund)

Jim _____
_____.
(enjoy + gerund)

Sharon _____
_____.
(not like + noun)

Jo _____
_____.
(enjoy + noun)

Grandma _____

_____ .

(like + noun)

Tom _____

_____ .

(like + to-infinitive)

❺ The following sentences have mistakes in them. Correct the highlighted sections. There may be more than one correct way to rewrite each sentence.

Example *My mother likes to romantic movies.*

→ *My mother likes to romantic movies.*
         ⌃
       watch

1 I really enjoy go to the beach.

_____

2 My friend Joe doesn't enjoy to dance.

_____

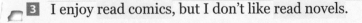

3 I enjoy read comics, but I don't like read novels.

_____

4 I don't think Jimmy likes study art. I think he likes to science class more.

_____

5 Jason enjoys to watch horror movies, but he doesn't like watch comedies.

_____

20

V. Now, Time to Speak!

6 Pair Work! Listen and practice the following dialogues. Then create similar conversations.

021

A

Man	I think that **hat** looks great on you.
Woman	Really? I don't like the **color**.
Man	Maybe you could try this **red** one then.
Woman	Yeah, OK. I really like that one.

hat →

jacket	suit	T-shirt	scarf
夾克	西裝	T 恤	圍巾

color →

pattern	size	style	fit
樣式	尺寸	風格	合身

red →

polka-dot	smaller	more modern	tighter
圓點	較小的	較現代的	較緊的

B

Man	How's your **steak**? Is it good?
Woman	No, I really don't like it. It's **undercooked**.
Man	Oh no! My **pasta** is delicious. It tastes amazing.
Woman	Can I eat some of yours? I love **Italian food**.
Man	Um, I'm not too keen on that idea.

steak /
pasta →

sushi	curry	fish and chips	paella
壽司	咖哩	炸魚和薯片	西班牙菜飯

undercooked →

cold	overcooked	too dry	too salty
冷的	煮太老的	太乾	太鹹

Italian food →

Japanese food	Indian food	English food	Spanish food
日本料理	印度料理	英國料理	西班牙料理

7 Ask your partner the following questions, and then fill in the chart. Report your findings to the class.

1 What kinds of movies do you like?

2 What foods do you love?

3 What foods don't you like?

4 What's your favorite class in school?

5 What do you like to do in your spare time?

Name _____

Favorite Kinds of Movies

_____

Favorite Foods

_____

Disliked Foods

_____

Favorite Class

_____

Favorite Hobbies

_____

8 Group Work! Write down three things you like and three things you dislike. Then find some classmates who share your likes and dislikes. Write extra information in the Comments section.

Example

You | Do you like horror movies, Bill?
Bill | Yes, I do. Japanese horror movies are my favorite.

Things I Like	Names of Classmates	Comments
Horror Movies	Bill	"Japanese horror movies are my favorite."

Things I Like	Names of Classmates	Comments

Things I Dislike	Names of Classmates	Comments

VI. Now, Time to Pronounce!

Fricative Consonants 擦音 [f] [v] [s] [z]

9 Listen and repeat the words that you hear.

(022) [f] fool fail faithful croft loafer

[v] vet vase vampire wives gave

(023) Say the following tongue twisters as many times as you can and as fast as possible.

The fruit fly feeds his flies on figs from France.
這隻果蠅用法國無花果餵食他的蒼蠅們。

Vets and valiant Vikings vie for velvet vases.
獸醫和英勇的維京人相爭天鵝絨花瓶。

10 Listen and repeat the words that you hear.

(024) [s] sofa sassy takes ghost lice

[z] zebra zeal has close prize

(025) Listen to the sentences and write [s] or [z] in the spaces given.

1 Zack is lazy, so he hates going swimming.
[z] [ ] [ ] [ ]

2 I like salsa, spaghetti, and jazz music.
[ ] [ ] [ ] [ ]

3 The shape of my nose makes me look wise.
[ ] [ ] [ ]

4 I detest people who sell laser guns.
[ ] [ ] [ ] [ ]

11 Listen to the words. Do you hear [f], [v], [s], or [z]? Write the words in the correct box.

(026)

1 fault   **5** hive   **9** wife

2 because   **6** is   **10** price

3 loose   **7** lose   **11** move

4 cellar   **8** living   **12** golf

[f]   [v]   [s]   [z]

23

Talking About Future Plans 談論未來計畫

I. Topic Preview 🎧 027

1 Inviting someone to a party 邀請某人參加派對

I'm having a party next week. Do you want to come?

Sure. I'll be there.

It's going to be so much fun.

I'll bring all my friends.

2 Talking about life after school 談論畢業後的生活

What are you planning on doing after graduating?

I'm planning on going traveling for a few months. You?

I'm getting a job at my dad's company.

3 Planning a trip 計畫旅行

I'm going on vacation next week.

How long are you going for?

I'm going for three weeks.

Where are you going?

I'm going to Spain for a week and then to France for two weeks.

4 Talking about holiday plans 談論節日計畫

What are your plans for Christmas?

I'm planning to spend time with my family.

5 Buying gifts for a friend's birthday 買生日禮物給朋友

Are you getting James something for his birthday?

Yes, I am. I'm going to buy him a gift tomorrow.

II. Vocabulary & Phrases 028

visit family 拜訪家人

go traveling 去旅行

go to university 上大學

work part-time 打工

play in a band 玩樂團

Europe 歐洲

Asia 亞洲

South America 南美州

Australia 澳洲

India 印度

a smartphone 一支智慧型手機

a watch 一支手錶

a bottle of wine 一瓶酒

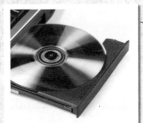
a DVD 一片DVD光碟

socks 襪子

Sentence Patterns 029

- _What_ are you _doing_ _this Saturday_? /
  What are you going to _do_ _this Saturday_?
  I'm _having_ _a party_. /
  I'm going to _have_ _a party_.
- _What_ are you planning on _doing_ _for Christmas_? /
  What are you planning to _do_ _for Christmas_?
  I'm planning on _visiting_ _my family_ _for Christmas_. /
  I'm planning to _visit_ _my family_ _for Christmas_.
- Are you _going traveling_ _this summer_? /
  Are you going to _go traveling_ _this summer_?
  Yes, I am. / No, I'm not.
- Are you planning on _working_ _after you graduate_? /
  Are you planning to _work_ _after you graduate_?
  Yes, I am. / No, I'm not.

Some time expressions that you can use when talking about the future:
談論未來事件常用的時間用語：

★ tomorrow	明天
★ next week	下週
★ this Saturday	這個星期六
★ next Saturday	下個星期六
★ next month	下個月
★ next year	明年
★ next summer	明年夏天
★ in two weeks' time	兩週
★ in six months' time	六個月

1 Listen to the following students talk about what they want to do when they leave school.
Match the speakers to the correct pictures.

(030)

1 _____

2 _____

3 _____

4 _____

5 _____

2 Listen to James talk about what he's planning to do next month. Then fill in the calendar.
One day has been filled in as an example.

(031)

1 _Sunday_	2 _Monday_	3 _Tuesday_	4 _Wednesday_	5 _Thursday_	6 _Friday_	7 _Saturday_
	play tennis with brother					

➡ (032) Now, listen to his vacation plans in Egypt, and put the events in the order that he plans to do them.

_1_

3 Sam and Lucy are talking about

(033) what birthday present to buy Emma.

Write the person's name under the

gift they plan to buy.

a

b

c

_____   _____   _____

➡ (034) Listen to the dialogue again. Fill in the blanks below with the words that you hear.

1 It's Emma's birthday _____. _____ you planning to get her?

2 I'm _____ get her a CD.

3 I'm either _____ her a book or a watch.

4 Oh no! Josh _____ to buy her a watch.

IV. Now, Grammar Time!

The Simple Future Tense
簡單未來式

Used For	Future Plans / Arrangements 未來計畫／安排		Offers / Predictions / Decisions / Requests 提供服務／預測／決定／要求
Affirmative Statements 肯定句	I am going to fix my car later.	I am fixing my car later.	I will fix the car for you! （我提供服務）
Negative Statements 否定句	He is not going to go to university.	He is not going to university.	He won't go to university. （我預測）
Yes/No Questions 是非問句	Are you going to work this summer? *Yes, I am. / No, I'm not.*	Are you working this summer? *Yes, I am. / No, I'm not.*	Will you work for me this summer? （我要求） *Yes, I will. / No, I won't.* （我決定）
WH-Questions WH 問句	What are they going to do this weekend?	What are they doing this weekend?	What will they choose to do? （你可以預測嗎？）

will is often shortened to 'll. ➔ I will = I'll

will not is often shortened to won't. ➔ I will not = I won't

4 Pair Work! Practice the following short conversations. Fill in the blanks with "be going to" or "will." The first dialogue has been completed for you.

1　A　Jack, I hear you <u>*are going to*</u> visit your family next week.

　　B　Yes, but I'm not sure on what date.

　　A　Well, there's no work on Tuesday because it's a holiday.

　　B　Oh, right. I <u>*will*</u> go on Tuesday then.

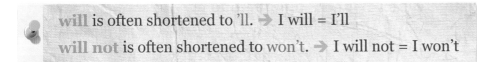

2　A　_____ you _____ come with us to the park

　　　tomorrow?

　　B　No, I _____ stay at home and finish my book.

3　A　Excuse me. _____ you help me open the window?

　　B　Sure, I _____ open it right away.

4 **A** Sarah, _____ you do me a favor?

B Sure. What's up?

A I _____ go shopping at one o'clock.

_____ you walk my dog?

B Oh, sorry. I can't. I _____ have lunch with

my boss.

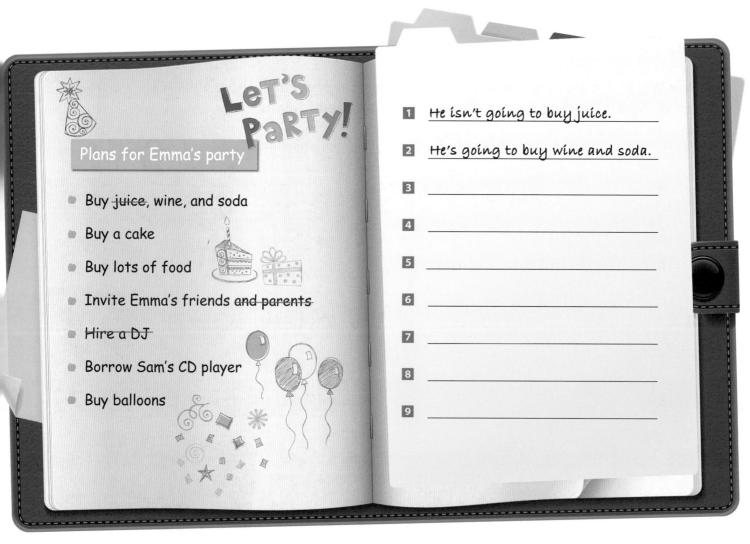

5 **A** Do you think it _____ rain tomorrow?

B I hope not, because I _____ go fishing

with my father.

5 Pair Work! Josh is planning a party for Emma. Look at his notes and take turns telling your partner what he's going to do and what he is not going to do.

LET'S PARTY!

Plans for Emma's party

- Buy ~~juice~~, wine, and soda
- Buy a cake
- Buy lots of food
- Invite Emma's friends ~~and parents~~
- ~~Hire a DJ~~
- Borrow Sam's CD player
- Buy balloons

1 He isn't going to buy juice.

2 He's going to buy wine and soda.

3 _____

4 _____

5 _____

6 _____

7 _____

8 _____

9 _____

V. Now, Time to Speak!

6 Ask your partner what his or her plans are for the holidays. You can use the model below. Report your findings to the class.

... *Halloween* ...
萬聖節

... *Christmas* ...
聖誕節

A | *What are you going to do for* **Halloween**?
B | *I'm going to* **dress up like a vampire and go to a Halloween party!**

Chinese New Year 中國新年

Mother's Day
母親節

7 Listen to the following conversations, and then practice them with your partner.

035 **1** A | I'm **having a Christmas party next week**. Do you want to come?
B | Sure. Thanks for inviting me. Where and when is it going to be?
A | It's going to be **at my house on the 24th of December**.
B | Do I need to bring anything?
A | Just bring **some gifts**. We're going to **exchange gifts at midnight**.

2 A | I'm planning on **going to a gig next weekend**. Do you want to join me?
B | Sure. Where is it going to be?
A | At **the nightclub on Albany Road**. **My favorite band is playing**.
B | Cool. Is anyone else going?
A | Yeah, **my sister's coming along** as well.

➡ Now, invite your partner to a party or special event. Talk about when and where the event will be, what you're planning to do there, and who's going with you.

EVENTS 活動

| a play 戲劇 | an opera 歌劇 | a baseball game 棒球賽 | a hockey game 曲棍球賽 | a gig 演唱會 |

| a movie night 電影之夜 | a pizza-eating contest 吃披薩大賽 | a comic convention 動漫展 | a dance class 舞蹈課 | a book signing 簽書會 |

Venues are on the next page. 場地請見下一頁 ↪

VENUES 場地

| a theater 劇院 | a concert hall 音樂廳 | a park 公園 | a stadium 體育場 | a nightclub 夜店 |
| a movie theater 電影院 | a restaurant 餐廳 | a community center 社區活動中心 | a school 學校 | a bookstore 書店 |

8 Take turns asking and answering the following questions with your partner. Ask a follow-up question for each one, too.

> **Example**
>
> A | *Where are you going on vacation next year?*
> B | *I'm going to Australia.*
> A | *What are you going to do there?*
> B | *I'm going to go surfing.*
> A | *How long are you going for?*
> B | *I'm going for three weeks.*

Note

If you don't have any plans, make a prediction/decision with "will."
如果你還沒有計畫，請用 will 來進行預測或做決定

A | *What are you going to do after class today?*
B | *I don't know. Maybe I'll go to McDonald's.*

1 Where are you going on vacation next year?

2 What are you planning to do after you graduate?

3 Are you going to do anything special for your birthday this year?

4 Are you going to any special events in the next few months?

5 What are you going to do after class today?

VI. Now, Time to Pronounce!

Fricative Consonants 擦音　[θ]　[ð]　[ʃ]　[ʒ]　[h]

9 Listen and repeat the words that you hear.

036

[θ]　　thing　thank　fourth　teeth　myth

[ð]　　this　smooth　then　these　weather

037　Now, listen and repeat the following sentences. Then write the <u>underlined</u> words in the correct box.

[θ]	[ð]
	There

→ <u>There</u> are <u>three</u> <u>toothbrushes</u> on my <u>brother's</u> desk.

→ <u>They</u> never <u>thought</u> about <u>the</u> <u>other</u>.

10 Listen and repeat the words that you hear.

038

[ʃ]　shape　passion　shine　shoal　fish

[ʒ]　garage　beige　vision　rouge　illusion

039　Now, try saying the following words aloud. Then listen and check your pronunciation. The sound has been colored for you.

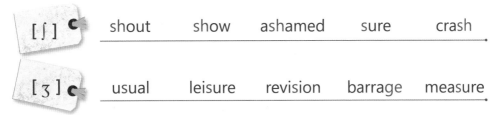

[ʃ]　shout　show　ashamed　sure　crash

[ʒ]　usual　leisure　revision　barrage　measure

11 Listen and repeat the words that you hear.

040

[h]　half　behind　head　happy　anyhow

041　Listen and circle the words that you hear.

1 heat | eat　　**2** hill | ill　　**3** harm | arm　　**4** hair | air　　**5** hedge | edge

31

I. Topic Preview (042)

1 *Talking about your sports team* 談論球隊

The Bears are a much better team than the Tigers. Our players are faster, stronger, and fitter than yours.

I totally disagree. The Tigers are the better team.
Yes, but our players have more heart.

2 *Asking for advice in a shop* 在商店內詢問他人建議

Excuse me. Which computer do you think is better?

Well, this one's faster and has more memory, but it's more expensive.

3 *Comparing people* 比較人物

Are you taller than Mike?

He's taller than me.

4 *Comparing places* 比較地點

How is Taiwan different from England?

Taiwan is much hotter than England, but the food is more delicious in Taiwan.

5 *Boasting* 自誇

I'm the smartest student in my class.

Nina says she's the fastest runner on the team.

Jack thinks he's the most talented actor in the world.

II. Vocabulary & Phrases

fast / faster / fastest
快的／較快的／最快的

heavy / heavier / heaviest
重的／較重的／最重的

old / older / oldest
年長的／較年長的／最年長的

young / younger / youngest
年輕的／較年輕的／最年輕的

beautiful / more beautiful / most beautiful
美麗的／較美麗的／最美麗的

smart / smarter / smartest
聰明的／較聰明的／最聰明的

interesting / more interesting / most interesting
有趣的／較有趣的／最有趣的

strong / stronger / strongest
強壯的／較強壯的／最強壯的

expensive / more expensive / most expensive
貴的／較貴的／最貴的

cheap / cheaper / cheapest
便宜的／較便宜的／最便宜的

convenient / more convenient / most convenient
方便的／較方便的／最方便的

hot / hotter / hottest
熱的／較熱的／最熱的

cold / colder / coldest
冷的／較冷的／最冷的

bad / worse / worst
差的／較差的／最差的

good / better / best
好的／較好的／最好的

Sentence Patterns

- I am _taller_ (than him).
- The book is _more interesting_ (than the movie).
- Tom and Jim are _older_ (than me).
- This smartphone is _faster_ (than that one).
- This computer has _more memory_ (than the other one).
- I have _more money_ (than you).
- Which team do you think is _better_?
- How is _Taiwan_ different from _Japan_? / How does _Taiwan_ compare to _Japan_?
- Is _India hotter_ than _England_?
- Are _you smarter_ than _Jenny_?
- I am the _handsomest boy_ in school.
- She is the _best tennis player_ in the world.

33

1 Listen to the following conversations. Then complete the sentences.

(045)

1 The man thinks the _____ shoes are better than the _____ shoes.

2 Jane says she's _____ than her father thinks.

3 The man and the woman are fighting about which _____ is _____.

4 The man thinks that Angelina Jolie is _____ actress in the United States.

5 The woman thinks she's _____ than everyone else.

2 Listen to the statements describing Daz, Simon, and Tom and then write the correct names in the boxes.

(046)

	180 cm	175 cm	173 cm
1 Height			
	80 kg	75 kg	60 kg
2 Weight			
	30	24	18
3 Age			
	130	120	100
4 IQ			

3 Listen to the people compare different items. Check ☑ the item that you think the speaker chooses each time.

(047)

1
a — vacation to Singapore
b — vacation to Japan

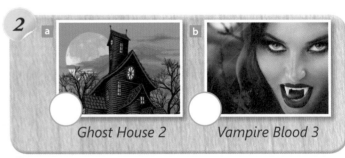

2
a — *Ghost House 2*
b — *Vampire Blood 3*

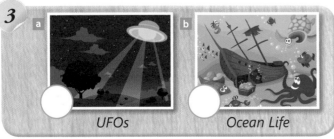

3
a — *UFOs*
b — *Ocean Life*

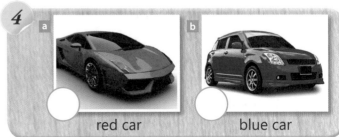

4
a — red car
b — blue car

IV. Now, Grammar Time!

Comparatives and Superlatives 比較級和最高級

	Comparatives 比較級	Superlatives 最高級
Short Adjectives 短形容詞	A horse is faster than a man.	Antarctica is the coldest place on earth.
Long Adjectives (more) 長形容詞（加 more）	My car is more expensive than yours.	The most convenient way to travel is by plane.
Long Adjectives (less) 長形容詞（加 less）	Your car is less expensive than mine.	The least convenient way to travel is on foot.
Irregular Adjectives (good, bad . . .) 不規則形容詞（more、bad 等）	My painting is better than yours.	Beyoncé is the best singer in the world.

Short Adjectives: Spelling Rules 短形容詞的拼寫規則

cold	(+er)	colder
safe	(+r)	safer
angry	(y+ier)	angrier
fat	(+_er)	fatter

4 Compare the objects in the pictures using the adjectives and prompts provided. The first sentence has been completed for you.

famous	colorful
dangerous	exciting
comfortable	angry

1 The shoes *are more colorful than* the jacket. *(more)*

2 The TV actor Bill Hader _____ than the movie star Hugh Jackman. *(less)*

3 Having a pet crocodile _____ _____ than having a pet cat. *(more)*

4 Reading a book _____ _____ than skydiving. *(less)*

5 The sofa _____ than the bed of nails. *(more)*

5 Look at the pictures, and then complete each sentence with a superlative adjective.

Mount Everest is 8,848 meters high.

1 Mount Everest is the

_____

mountain on earth.

Usain Bolt ran the 100m in 9.58 seconds.

2 As of May 2013,

Usain Bolt is the

_____

man in the world.

Bill Gates has $72,700,000,000.

3 As of May 2013,

Bill Gates is the world's

_____ man.

Sultan Kösen is 251 cm tall.
(cc by Amsterdamman)

4 As of May 2013,

Sultan Kösen is the

_____

man in the world.

Christopher Plummer was 87 years old when he won the Academy Award in 2012.

5 As of May 2013,

Christopher Plummer is the

_____

Academy Award winner.

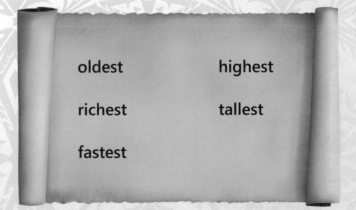

oldest   highest

richest   tallest

fastest

V. Now, Time to Speak!

6 Pair Work! Look at the information tables and take turns comparing the two countries. Use the adjectives in the box below.

| hot | wet | populated | big / large | rich / wealthy | |

A | The United Kingdom has an **average temperature** of 15 degrees.
B | India has an **average temperature** of 35 degrees.
A | So, India is **hotter** than the United Kingdom.

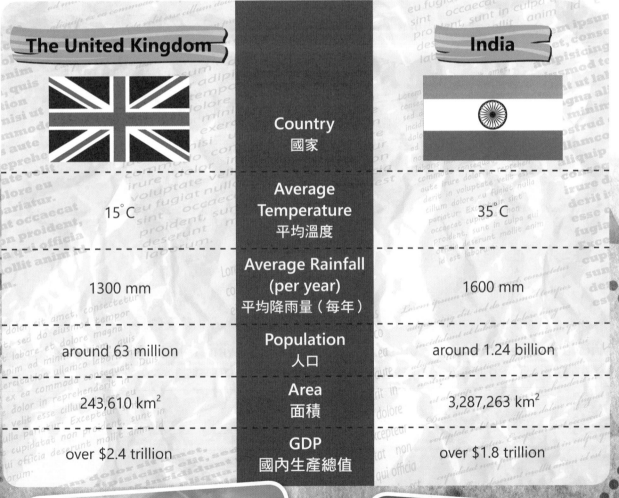

The United Kingdom	Country 國家	India
15°C	Average Temperature 平均溫度	35°C
1300 mm	Average Rainfall (per year) 平均降雨量（每年）	1600 mm
around 63 million	Population 人口	around 1.24 billion
243,610 km²	Area 面積	3,287,263 km²
over $2.4 trillion	GDP 國內生產總值	over $1.8 trillion

7 Group Work! Two students should play the roles of salespeople and try to sell the products below to a third student. Change roles for each pair of products.

Salesman A	You should buy this hat because it's **more stylish**.
Salesman B	Yes, but this one is **more colorful**.
Salesman A	This one's **cheaper**.
Customer	Hmm. I think I'll take the **colorful one**.

More Adjectives
更多形容詞

powerful 有力量的

cool 酷的

useful 實用的

professional 專業的

stylish 時髦的

elegant 優雅的

valuable 貴重的

economical 經濟實惠的

1 A | You should buy this motorcycle

because it's _____.

2 A | You should buy this watch

because it's _____.

3 A | You should buy this coat

because it's _____.

8 With a partner, take turns boasting about the following things. Make comparisons to prove it. Then tell the class about your partner's boasts.

Example

I'm the smartest man in the world. My brain is bigger than a basketball!

best singer | handsomest man / most beautiful woman | richest | smartest | best athlete

38

VI. Now, Time to Pronounce!

Stop Consonants 阻音   [p] [b] [t] [d]

9 Listen and repeat the words that you hear.

(048)

[p]   please   help   reap   peel   happy

[b]   boy   block   table   rub   bile

(049) Listen and (circle) the words that you hear.

1 breeze | peas **2** bile | pile **3** cab | cap **4** bear | pear **5** pill | bill

10 Listen and repeat the words that you hear.

(050)

[t]   talk   tea   eating   tall   beat

[d]   den   added   dean   fend   land

(051) Try to pronounce the words by yourself. Then listen and check your pronunciation.

1 deem **6** lend
2 dealer **7** friend
3 tent **8** dent
4 banter **9** team
5 bend **10** salt

11 Listen to the words. Do you (052) hear [p], [b], [t], or [d]? Check ☑ the box that corresponds to the sound that you hear.

	[p]	[b]	[t]	[d]
1.				
2.				
3.				
4.				
5.				
6.				
7.				
8.				

Talking About People You Know
談論你所認識的人

I. Topic Preview (053)

1 How you know a mutual friend
你如何認識某位共同朋友

Hi, I think we have a mutual friend. Peter Jones. I think he works with you. He's my brother-in-law.

Oh really? Who?
Yes! How do you know him?

2 Gossiping 八卦

Did you hear the news about Simon?

No. What happened?

He left his job and went to live in Antarctica!

3 Discussing a friend's problems
討論某位朋友的問題

How's Anthony's mother? I heard she's not well.

Yeah, she hurt herself pretty badly.

4 Recommending a friend 推薦朋友

I need to find a singer for my band. Can he sing?

How about my friend Daniel?
Yeah, he sings beautifully.

II. Vocabulary & Phrases (054)

colleague 同事

neighbor 鄰居

friend of the family 家族朋友

distant relative 遠親

classmate 同學

teammate 隊友

regular customer 常客

babysitter 褓姆

roommate 室友

hairdresser 美髮師

dump his girlfriend / her boyfriend 甩了他女友／她男友

have a baby 生小孩

get arrested 被捕

have an accident 出車禍

lose his/her job
被炒魷魚

Sentence Patterns (055)

- We have a mutual friend.
- How do you know _Jane_?
- _Bradley's_ my _colleague_. We _play soccer_ together.
  Jasmine's a _friend_ of mine. I know her from my _dance class_.
- Did you hear the news about _Paul_?

- What happened? / Give me the gossip!
- Apparently, _John's uncle_ _got arrested_.
  I heard _Liz_ _had an accident_.
- I need to find a _roommate_.
  How about my _colleague Jeremy_?

Now, Time to Listen!

1 How does Bill know the people in the table? Listen to the conversations and check ☑ the correct box. The first row has been completed for you.

(056)

People Bill Knows

		colleague	babysitter	roommate	friend of the family	distant relative
1	Sam Crooks			✓		
2	Peter Smith					
3	Nick Brown					
4	Robert Wells					
5	Jenny Bond					

2 Listen to these short extracts. Decide whether the people are gossiping (G), recommending a friend (R), discussing a friend's problems (D), or talking about how they know a mutual friend (M).

(057)

1	R	2		3		4	
5		6		7		8	

3 Listen to Sarah's friends talk about her. Check ☑ the pictures that best describe Sarah. You may need to check more than one box for each part.

(058)

42

IV. Now, Grammar Time!

Adverbs and Adjectives
副詞和形容詞

To form an adverb, add -ly to the adjective. 在形容詞的字尾加 **ly** 可構成副詞	
Adjective 形容詞 describing a noun 修飾名詞	**Adverb 副詞** describing a verb 修飾動詞
He's a careful <u>worker</u>. →	He <u>works</u> carefully.
She's a slow <u>runner</u>. →	She <u>runs</u> slowly.

Forming Adverbs 構成副詞:
Spelling Rules 拼寫規則

loud	(+ly)	loud<u>ly</u>
beautiful	(+ly)	beautiful<u>ly</u>
lazy	(y+ily)	laz<u>ily</u>
terrible	(e+y)	terrib<u>ly</u>
energetic	(+ally)	energetic<u>ally</u>

Irregular Adverbs 不規則副詞	• good → well • hard → hard • fast → fast • late → late • early → early

4 Complete the following sentences using adverbs. The first sentence has been completed for you.

1 John is a terrible singer. He sings <u>terribly</u>.

2 Max is a messy writer. He writes _____.

3 Jenny thinks math is easy. She does her homework _____.

4 Sarah is a safe driver. She drives _____.

5 Matt is a very patient person. He always waits _____.

6 These are automatic doors. They open _____.

7 Ben is a good dog. He behaves _____.

8 Lucy has a loud voice. She speaks very _____.

5 Look at the pictures and then use adverbs to complete the table about James. There may be more than one correct answer for each picture. Compare your answers with the class.

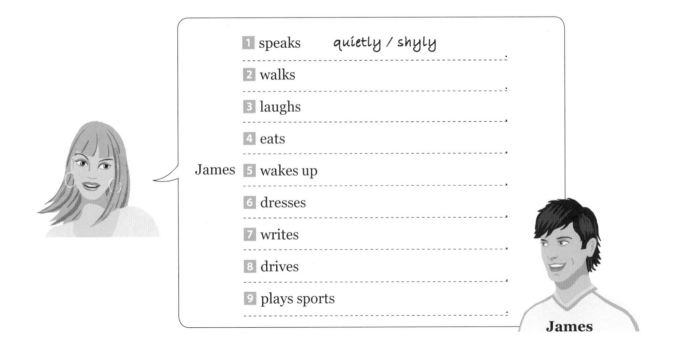

James

1 speaks	*quietly / shyly*	
2 walks		
3 laughs		
4 eats		
5 wakes up		
6 dresses		
7 writes		
8 drives		
9 plays sports		

James

V. Now, Time to Speak!

6 Pair Work! Listen to the dialogue and practice it with your partner.
Then create similar dialogues using the pictures given.

(059)

A

A	Do you know anyone who can **fix a computer**?
B	Yes, my **friend Bob** can. He **fixes computers** really **quickly**.

dance enthusiastically

act professionally

drive a bus safely

 (060) Now, let's try another one!

B

A	Do you know **Dan Jones**?
B	Yes, he's my **teammate**. I know him from **soccer practice**. How do you know him?
A	He's my **colleague**. **We work together**.

customer

hairdresser

neighbor

distant relative

classmate

roommate

7 Fill in the table about someone both you and your partner know well. Then describe that person to your partner. Can your partner guess the person?

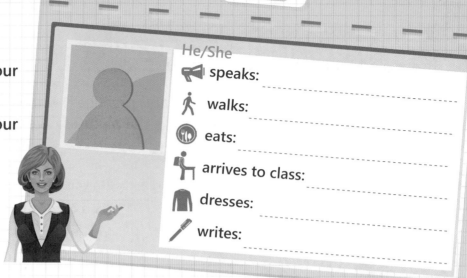

He/She

speaks: _____

walks: _____

eats: _____

arrives to class: _____

dresses: _____

writes: _____

8 Listen to the following conversation and practice it with your partner.

061

Jeremy	**Mindy**, did you hear about **Ben**?
Mindy	No. What happened?
Jeremy	I heard he **dumped his girlfriend**.
Mindy	No way! He told me last week he wanted to marry her!
Jeremy	Well, apparently **last night he went to James's party with another girl**.
Mindy	Oh my God!

➤ Now, choose one of the topics below and gossip about it with your partner. Report the gossip you heard to the class.

| Your friend got arrested. | Your friend had an accident. | Your friend got fired. |

Phrases to help you gossip 聊八卦的用語：

Crimes 犯罪	steal something 偷竊	 hit someone 打人	 drive dangerously 危險駕駛	 jaywalk 穿越馬路
Accidents 意外	 be hit by a car 被車撞	 fall down the stairs 跌落樓梯	 slip on the sidewalk 在人行道上滑倒	 burn oneself 燙傷自己
Reasons for Getting Fired 被炒魷魚的理由	 argue with the boss 和老闆吵架	 turn up late for work 上班遲到	 fall asleep at work 上班時睡著	 take a three-hour lunch break 中午休了三個小時

VI. Now, Time to Pronounce!

Stop Consonants 阻音   [k]   [g]   [tʃ]   [dʒ]

9 Listen and repeat the words that you hear.

062

[k]   key   cold   calf   lock   wake

[g]   give   ago   golf   flag   pig

063   Listen and repeat the following sentences. Circle all the words that contain the [k] sound.

I keep the girl's gold in the kitchen cupboard.

You can play golf in my garden, but be careful of the pink gate.

064   Now, listen again and underline all the words that contain the [g] sound.

10 Listen and repeat the words that you hear.

065

[tʃ]   chop   chess   watch   blotch   cheer

[dʒ]   job   page   jewel   gem   gentle

066   Listen to the words. Do you hear [tʃ] or [dʒ]? Check ☑ the box that corresponds to the sound that you hear.

	[tʃ]	[dʒ]
1.		
2.		
3.		
4.		
5.		
6.		

Shopping 購物

I. Topic Preview (067)

1 Finding something in a supermarket 在超市裡找東西

Excuse me. Where can I find the fresh fruit?
Thank you. Oh, do you have any shampoo in stock?

Fresh fruit is on aisle five. I'll show you.
No, I'm sorry. We're sold out.

2 Asking for a different size 要求其他尺寸

Can I try this in a bigger size?

Of course. What size do you want to try?

Size 12, please.

3 Asking for a different color 要求其他顏色

Do you have this in a different color?

What color do you want to try?

Green, please.

4 Bargaining at the market 在市場殺價

How much is this?

That's $100.

That's way too expensive. I'll give you $50 for it.

$50? It's worth at least $75.

OK, deal.

5 Paying at the checkout counter 在收銀台結帳

That'll be $52, sir. Cash or credit card?

Credit card, please.

6 Asking for a refund 要求退貨

Hello. I want to return this sweater.
Yes, here you go. Can I get a refund?

OK. Do you have the receipt?
No, I'm sorry. But you can exchange it for another sweater.

II. Vocabulary & Phrases

dried food 乾貨

frozen food 冷凍食品

toiletries 盥洗用品

makeup 化妝品

men's clothes 男裝

electronic goods 電子商品

aisle 走道

checkout counter 收銀台

top shelf 上層

middle shelf 中層

bottom shelf 下層

exchange 換貨

refund 退貨

receipt 收據

credit card / debit card 信用卡

cash 現金

line / queue 排隊

Sentence Patterns

* Where can I find the *toiletries*?
  Where is/are the *frozen food/electronic goods*?
  It's/They're on aisle *three*.
* Do you have any *shampoo* in stock?
  Sorry. We're sold out.
* Can I try this in a different *color*?
* Do you have this in a different *size*?
* What *color* do you want to try?
  Blue, please.
* How much is this/are these?
  It's/They're *$20*.

* That's too *expensive*!
  That's very *reasonable*!
* How do you want to pay?
  With *cash*, please.
* I want to return these *shoes*.
* It's/They're too small.
  It's/They're broken.
* Can I get a refund?
* I have the receipt here.

1 Lucy is at the supermarket. Listen to the conversations she has and check ☑ True or False.

(070)

A

True	False	
_____	_____	**1** Lucy wants to buy some frozen food.
_____	_____	**2** Lucy can find what she wants on aisle seven.
_____	_____	**3** The item Lucy wants is on the bottom shelf.

B

True	False	
_____	_____	**1** Lucy's at the checkout counter.
_____	_____	**2** She wants to get a refund.
_____	_____	**3** She has the receipt with her.

2 Listen to the following conversations that you might hear in a shop. Then match each conversation to the correct picture.

(071)

3 Listen to the short conversations and fill in the blanks.

(072)

1 A   Excuse me. _____ is this DVD player?

     B   It's $200, but it's the newest model.

     A   Oh, actually I think that's very _____.

2 A   Excuse me. Do you have any toothpaste _____?

     B   Yes, the toothpaste should be _____ two.

     A   I looked there, but I didn't find any.

     B   Oh, it's on the _____. It's a little hard to see.

3 A   Hello. I'm _____ some apples.

     B   I'm sorry. We're _____ of apples right now.

4 A   This dress is very nice. Do you have it in a _____?

     B   Yes, of course. What size do you want to _____?

     A   Size _____, please.

     B   OK. I'll get one for you now.

5 A   I _____ this T-shirt here yesterday, but it has holes in it.

     B   Oh, I'm sorry. If you have the _____, I can give you _____.

IV. Now, Grammar Time!

These conjunctions connect words, phrases, and clauses.
用來連接單字、片語或字句的連接詞

for giving a reason 提出原因	I took the shirt back to the shop, for it was too small.
and adding one thing to another 附加事物	I want to buy some makeup and a new scarf.
nor expressing "and not" 表達「也不」	He doesn't have any cash, nor does he have a credit card.
but contrasting 對比	John wanted to go to the movies, but Jane wanted to go shopping.
or giving options 提供選擇	Would you like a size 12 or a size 13?
yet expressing "nevertheless" 表達「然而」	I told him I wanted blue shoes, yet he still bought me black ones.
so giving a result 提出結果	James needed money, so he went to work in a shop.

Note **And**, **but**, **or**, and **so** are the most commonly used conjunctions.
and、but、or 和 so 是最常用的連接詞

4 Pair Work! Look at the pictures and fill in the blanks. You'll need to use "or," "and," "but," or "so."

5 Pair Work! Take turns combining each pair of sentences below into a single sentence by using a conjunction. The first pair has been combined for you as an example.

1 James wants to buy a CD. He wants to buy a DVD.

James wants to buy a CD and a DVD.

2 Lucy likes the yellow boots. She doesn't like the red ones.

_____

3 Tom kept his receipt. He can get a refund.

_____

4 Jane has $10. Shampoo is $7, and toothpaste is $8.

Jane can buy _____

5 Rob doesn't want the jeans. He doesn't want the sweater.

_____

6 I had the receipt. They still didn't give me a refund.

_____

7 I can't show you any different sizes. We don't have any in stock.

_____

8 Toiletries are on aisle five. Makeup is on aisle six.

_____

V. Now, Time to Speak!

6 Pair Work! Listen to the dialogues and practice them with your partner. Then create new dialogues by replacing the words in bold with words of your choice.

(073)

A

A	Excuse me. I'm trying to find the **eyeliner**.
B	The **eyeliner** is on **aisle six**.
A	Thank you.

hair dye
染髮劑

potato chips
洋芋片

camping equipment
露營裝備

stationery
文具

instant coffee
即溶咖啡

B

A	Excuse me. Can I try on **this T-shirt**?
B	Of course. The changing rooms are over there.
A	**It's** a little too **big**. Do you have it in a different **size**?

dress 洋裝

skirt 裙子

gloves 手套

waistcoat/ vest 背心

tie 領帶

tight 緊身的

baggy 寬鬆的

short 短的

long 長的

old-fashioned
老派的

Reminder You can find more useful vocabulary in Unit 2.

C

A	Excuse me. How much **is this watch**?
B	**It's $100**.
A	Wow! That's very **expensive**. I'll give you **$30** for it.

designer bag
設計師包包／名牌包

fur boots
毛靴

cufflinks
袖扣

laptop
筆記型電腦

MP3 player
MP3 播放器

7 Look at the pictures. Discuss with a partner what the people in the pictures might be saying. Then share your ideas with the class.

Example *In this picture, I think the man is saying, "I bought this yesterday, but it's broken."*

➡ Now, try these two pictures!

$5?
$6?

$10?
$7.5?

8 Listen to the dialogue, and then practice it with your partner.

Shop Owner	Hello. Do you see anything you like?
Customer	Yes, I quite like **this teapot**.
Shop Owner	Oh, yes. It's very **beautiful**, isn't it?
Customer	How much is it?
Shop Owner	It's **$50**.
Customer	That's far too expensive!
Shop Owner	**But this teapot is over 70 years old, sir.**
Customer	I won't pay **$50** for it. I'll give you **$10**.
Shop Owner	It's worth at least **$40**.
Customer	OK, how about **$30**.
Shop Owner	I won't go lower than **$35**. Look at how **pretty the color is**.
Customer	OK, here you go—**$35**.

➡ Now, role-play a similar situation using the items below. One student should play a customer and the other should play a shop owner. Who is better at bargaining? Tell the class.

statuette
小雕像

Persian rug
波斯地毯

bottle of perfume
香水

oil painting
油畫

notebook
筆記本

Ⅵ Now, Time to Pronounce!

Nasal Consonants 鼻音   [m]   [n]   [ŋ]

9 Listen and repeat the words that you hear.

(075)

[m]   melt   mire   slim   calm   amount

[n]   nose   near   sun   know   grin

(076) ➡ Listen and ⓒircle the words that you hear.

1 melt | knelt   **2** grim | grin   **3** mow | know   **4** sum | sun   **5** mill | nil

10 Listen to the following tongue twisters. Then try to say them as many times as you

(077) can and as fast as possible.

Mary's Mother's making Mary marry me.
瑪麗的媽媽要瑪麗嫁給我。

No one knows a nicer gnome than Ned.
沒有人認識比奈德更好心的矮人。

11 Listen and repeat the words that you hear.

(078)

[ŋ]   sing   rang   finger   drink   sank

(079) ➡ The following words contain either an [n] sound or an [ŋ] sound.
Listen and ⓒircle the words that have an [ŋ] sound.

1 don   **2** hinge   **3** knight   **4** spring   **5** mink   **6** dangle

7 wring   **8** think   **9** lank   **10** single   **11** glint   **12** lend

12 Listen and repeat the following sentences. Then write the correct phonetic symbol—

(080) [m], [n], or [ŋ]—in the spaces given.

1 Nora the singer is my best friend.
[　]　　[　]　[　]　　　[　]

2 Jimmy never knocks before entering.
[　][　]　[　]　　　　[　]

3 This African bird has pink fringes on its wings.
[　]　　　　[　][　]　　　　[　]

4 Sinbad knows his ship might sink.
[　]　[　]　　　　[　]　　[　]

Emergencies
緊急事件

I. Topic Preview 🎧 081

1 *Calling an ambulance* 叫救護車

This is 911. What's your emergency?

My father is having a heart attack.

What's your address?

Twenty-one Pine Avenue.

The paramedics will be there soon.

2 *Calling the police* 報警

This is 911. What's your emergency? Are you hurt?

Someone just stole my bag.
No, I'm fine. I'm outside number three Oak Boulevard.

We're sending the police now.

3 *Calling the fire department* 叫消防隊

Hello? Is this 911? My house is on fire.
No, I'm outside.
Forty-five Holly Drive.

Stay calm. Are you inside the house now?
Do not go back in.
What's your address?
The fire department is on the way.

4 *Asking passersby for medical assistance* 請路人提供醫療協助

Help! Can someone please help me?

What's the problem?

My son is choking!

It's OK. I know the Heimlich maneuver.

II. Vocabulary & Phrases 〔082〕

have a heart attack 心臟病發

have an allergic reaction 過敏

be attacked 受到攻擊

drown 溺水

choke 噎到

paramedics 醫務人員

fire department 消防隊

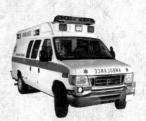

ambulance 救護車

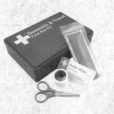

first aid 急救箱

police 警察

(do) the Heimlich maneuver
（施行）哈姆立克急救法

(do) CPR
（施行）心肺復甦術

clean a wound
清理傷口

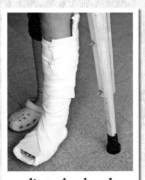

splint a broken leg
用夾板將斷腿固定

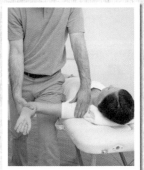

relocate a shoulder
將肩部復位

Sentence Patterns 〔083〕

- What's your emergency?
  What's the problem?
  My *sister* is *drowning*.
  I'm *having an allergic reaction*.
  I *was attacked*.
  Someone stole my *phone*.
- What's your address? / Where are you?
- Stay calm. / It's OK. / Are you hurt?

- *An ambulance* is on the way.
- Does anyone here know *first aid*?
  Does anyone here know how to *splint a broken leg*?
- Can anyone here *relocate a shoulder*?
  Is anyone here a doctor?
- I know *first aid*. /
  I know how to *clean a wound*.
- Please help me! / I need help! /
  Can someone please help me?

III. Now, Time to Listen!

1 Listen to the 911 calls. For each one, check ☑ the pictures that match the content
of the conversation most accurately. You may need to check more than one correct
answer in each conversation.

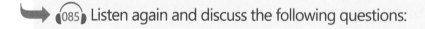

(085) Listen again and discuss the following questions:

★ Which of the calls were emergency calls?

★ What kinds of emergencies were there?

★ Were some of the emergencies more serious than others?

★ How did the 911 operator speak?

★ What would you do if you were the person in Conversation 3?

2 Listen to the 911 call, and then put the conversation in the correct order by writing numbers 1-9 in the spaces given. The first sentence has been numbered for you.

(086)

_1_____ Nine-one-one. What's your emergency?

_____ Yes. What should I do now?

_____ OK. Stay calm. What's your address?

_____ Stay on the phone. The police will be there in two minutes.

_____ It's 53 North Road. Please, send the police quickly.

_____ The police are on their way. Are you in your bedroom?

_____ Yes, I am. The burglar is downstairs in the living room.

_____ Help! Someone's in my house! I think it's a burglar.

_____ Stay in your bedroom. Can you lock the door?

3 Listen to the following people in emergency situations. Match the beginning of each conversation with the correct response.

(087)

1 • **a** Stand back everyone. I know CPR!

2 • **b** Yes, I know how to clean a wound.

3 • **c** Don't worry. I can relocate your shoulder in no time.

4 • **d** Tell us where you are, and we'll send an ambulance.

5 • **e** Yes. What's your emergency?

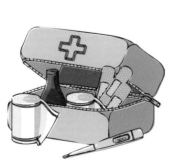

IV. Now, Grammar Time!

> **Linking Verbs** 連綴動詞
> Linking verbs connect the subject to information about the subject.
> 連綴動詞用來連接主詞與其相關說明

Verb 動詞	Describing the Subject Using an Adjective 用形容詞來描述主詞	Describing the Subject Using a Noun/Clause 用名詞或子句來描述主詞
be (am/is/are/was/were…)	John is ill.	John is like a brother to me.
look 看起來	You look tired.	You look like hell.
smell 聞起來	Your perfume smells nice.	Her house smells like fresh flowers.
feel 感覺	My leg feels very sore.	My head feels like it's going to explode.
sound 聽起來	Kate sounds very happy this morning.	Jane sounds like she has the flu.
seem 似乎	Your cold seems better today.	You seem like there's something wrong.
taste 嚐起來	This sandwich tastes a bit strange.	This ice cream tastes like heaven.

❹ Pair Work! Complete the short dialogues below using a linking verb or linking verb + like. The first dialogue has been completed as an example.

1　A　You <u>look</u> ill today Pete. Are you feeling OK?

　　B　No, I <u> feel like </u> I'm going to faint.

2　A　 Oh no! Is your leg OK? It _____ it's broken.

　　B　Argh! It hurts so much. It _____ so painful.

3　A　Help! I'm choking!

　　B　Sam! Sam! What's wrong? I can't understand you.

　　C　It _____ he's choking! Someone do the Heimlich maneuver!

4　A　Can you smell something? Something _____ very strange.

　　B　Yes. It _____ smoke. Oh no! The house is on fire!

5　A　Help! My brother won't wake up. He _____ cold. What's wrong with him?

　　B　Don't panic. Is he breathing? Put your ear next to his mouth.

　　A　Yes, he's breathing, but his breathing _____ very painful.

5 Complete the descriptions of the pictures using the words provided.

feels   looks like   being attacked   seems like   looks   sounds like

red   a cold   smells like   hot   burning   drowning

Grandpa says he _____

_____ and faint.

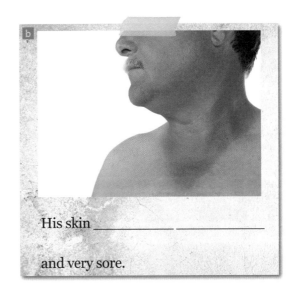

His skin _____ _____

and very sore.

It _____ someone's

_____.

It _____ something's

_____ in the kitchen.

It _____ that

man's _____!

It _____ _____,

but it might be a rare disease.

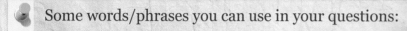

V. Now, Time to Speak!

6 Pair Work! Look at the pictures on page 63 and decide what questions a 911 operator needs to ask in each situation. Discuss your ideas with the class.

Some words/phrases you can use in your questions:

swell up / swollen
腫起來／浮腫的

be trapped
被陷阱困住

a weapon
武器

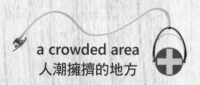

a crowded area
人潮擁擠的地方

feel dizzy
頭昏

Fire

a

Are you inside the house?

Medical emergency

b

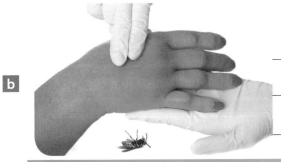

Is the wound red or painful?

Police call

c

Are you in danger right now?

POLICE

Role-play! Choose one of the situations mentioned above. Student A should play the 911 operator and Student B should play the caller. Use the model below to start each call.

Student A	*Nine-one-one, What's your emergency?*
Student B	**My house is on fire!**
Student A	*OK. What's your address? / Where are you?*
Student B	*I'm at **67 Oak Street**.*
Student A	**Are you inside the house?**

7 Listen to the dialogue below and practice it with your partner. Then have similar conversations by replacing the phrases in color with ones from the word bank.

(088)

WORD BANK

- dislocated his/her shoulder playing soccer
- is choking
- broke his/her leg
- cut his/her hand on glass
- had a heart attack
- isn't breathing

- the Heimlich maneuver
- CPR
- first aid

- clean a wound
- relocate a shoulder
- splint a broken leg
- save him/her
- help

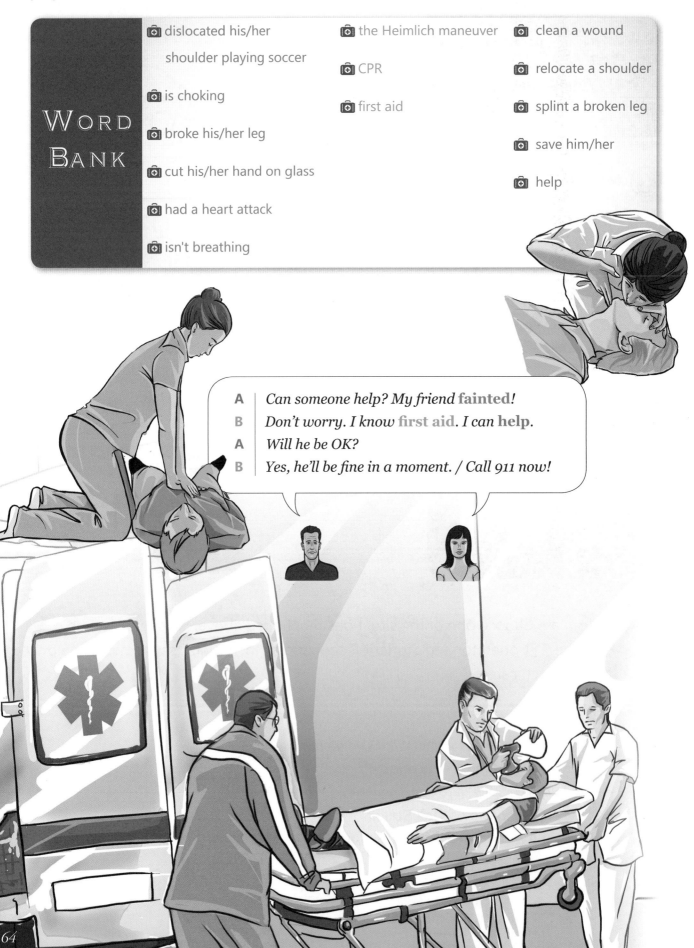

A	Can someone help? My friend **fainted**!
B	Don't worry. I know **first aid**. I can **help**.
A	Will he be OK?
B	Yes, he'll be fine in a moment. / Call 911 now!

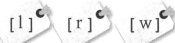

VI. Now, Time to Pronounce!

Lateral & Gliding Consonants 邊音與滑音 [l] [r] [w] [j]

8 Listen and repeat the words that you hear.

089

[l]

| left | line | while | child | lane |

[r]

| rent | rod | virus | far | rice |

090 Listen and circle the words that you hear.

1 wire | while **2** rip | lip **3** roam | loam **4** red | led **5** road | load

091 Listen to the words and check ☑ the correct box.

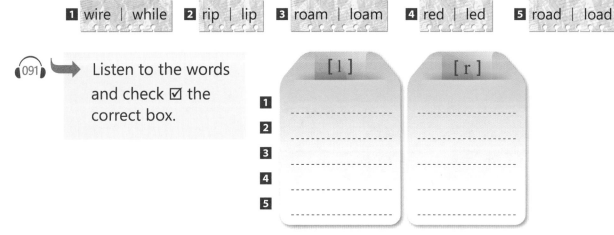

	[l]	[r]
1		
2		
3		
4		
5		

9 Listen and repeat the words that you hear.

092

[w]

| water | whale | went | forward | always |

[j]

| yes | your | opinion | yard | yell |

10 Listen to the following tongue twisters. Then try to say them as many times as you can
093 and as fast as possible.

Yes, we're yelling for your yellow yoyo.
是的，我們就是在為你的黃色溜溜球歡呼。

Which wicked witch wished the wicked wish?
哪一個邪惡的女巫許了這個邪惡的願望？

Talking on the Phone 打電話

I. Topic Preview 094

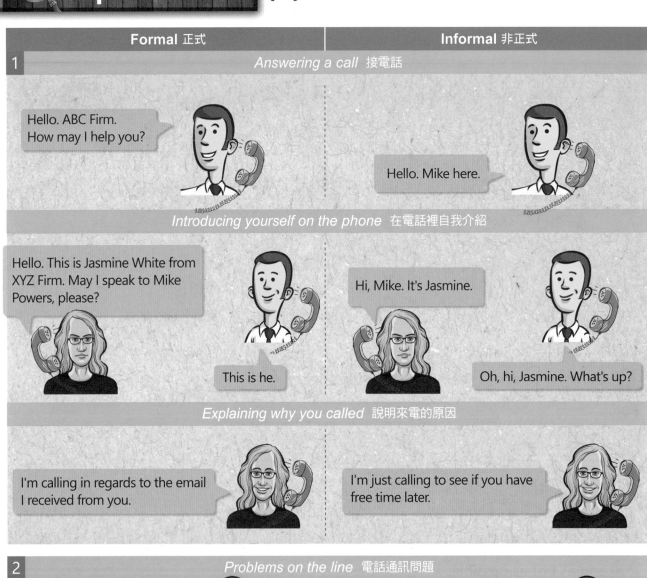

Formal 正式	Informal 非正式

1 Answering a call 接電話

Hello. ABC Firm. How may I help you?

Hello. Mike here.

Introducing yourself on the phone 在電話裡自我介紹

Hello. This is Jasmine White from XYZ Firm. May I speak to Mike Powers, please?

This is he.

Hi, Mike. It's Jasmine.

Oh, hi, Jasmine. What's up?

Explaining why you called 說明來電的原因

I'm calling in regards to the email I received from you.

I'm just calling to see if you have free time later.

2 Problems on the line 電話通訊問題

Hello. Is this Mike Powers?

I'm sorry. I think you have the wrong number.

Hello. Can you hear me?

I'm sorry. You're breaking up. The signal is very bad.

3 Ending a conversation 結束對話

Thank you very much for your time. Goodbye.

Talk to you later. Bye.

II. Vocabulary & Phrases (095)

put someone on hold
請某人稍等

transfer the call
轉接電話

have a chat
聊天

leave/take a message
留言／記錄留言

make an appointment
約時間

call in sick
打電話請病假

make a complaint
抱怨

place an order
訂產品

make a reservation
預約；訂位

arrange a meeting
安排會議

arrange an interview
安排面試

reschedule an interview
面試時間改期

a bad signal
收訊不良

hang up 掛斷

the wrong number
錯誤的電話號碼

Sentence Patterns (096)

- This is *Jack White*.
  Jack White speaking.
  Hi, *Jack* here.
- How may I help you?
  May I speak to *Mary Powers*, please?
  Is *Mary* there?
  Is this *Mary*?
  This is *she*. / Speaking.
- Let me *put you on hold*.
  Wait a moment.
  I'll just *transfer the call*.

- I'm calling in regards to *the interview*.
  I'm calling to discuss *your order*.
  I'm calling because *I'm going to be late*.
  I'm just ringing to *arrange a meeting*.
- Can you *take a message* for me?
  Do you want to *leave a message*?
- I'm sorry. I think you have the wrong number.
- I can't hear you. There's a bad signal.
  You're breaking up.
- Thanks for your time.
  Thanks for calling.
  I'll speak to you soon.

III. Now, Time to Listen!

1 Listen to the following phone conversations and check ☑ the correct answers.

A
(097)

1 The caller's name is _____.

- [ ] **a** David Price
- [ ] **b** Simon Jones
- [ ] **c** Simon Price

2 The caller is calling because _____.

- [ ] **a** he wants to discuss an order
- [ ] **b** he wants to reschedule an interview
- [ ] **c** he wants to chat

3 The caller is now going to _____.

- [ ] **a** speak to the boss's secretary
- [ ] **b** leave a message
- [ ] **c** hang up

B
(098)

1 Joe is probably Maria's _____.

- [ ] **a** boss
- [ ] **b** doctor
- [ ] **c** friend

2 Maria is calling Joe to _____.

- [ ] **a** arrange to meet up
- [ ] **b** make a reservation
- [ ] **c** discuss a problem

3 Joe wants Maria to _____.

- [ ] **a** transfer his call
- [ ] **b** pay for dinner
- [ ] **c** call him again later

2 Listen to Matt's four conversations. Match each conversation to the person he's calling and the subject of his conversation.
(099)

①   ②   ③   ④

a — store manager ✿

b — ✿ doctor's office

c — hotel reception ✿

d — ✿ secretary

| **1** make an appointment | **2** call in sick | **3** arrange an interview | **4** make a complaint |

3 Listen to Sam Black from Peartree Publishing talk to Jo Bennett's secretary at the Woodstock Paper Company. Then check ☑ True or False.
(100)

True	False	
_____	_____	**1** Jo is in the office.
_____	_____	**2** Sam wants to leave a message.
_____	_____	**3** Sam wants to reschedule a meeting.
_____	_____	**4** Sam wants to place an order.
_____	_____	**5** Sam wants Jo to call him tomorrow.

IV. Now, Grammar Time!

Gerunds and Infinitives
are verbs that can act like nouns.
動名詞與不定詞
是可作名詞使用的動詞。

Note In conversational English, it's much more common to use the gerund than the infinitive as a subject.
在英語對話中，較常用動名詞作主詞，而少用不定詞作主詞。
→ ~~To read~~ Reading is my favorite hobby.

	Gerund = [verb]-ing 動名詞 = 動詞 +ing	Infinitive = to + [verb] 不定詞 = to+ 動詞
Used as a subject 作主詞	Leaving a message is very easy.	To leave a message is very easy.
Used as an object 作受詞	I like chatting with you.	I like to chat with you.

Some verbs take a gerund as an object. 有些動詞必須接動名詞為受詞	enjoy / finish / discuss / dislike / recommend / don't mind I recommend talking to the manager about that problem. Let's discuss meeting up next week.
Some verbs take an infinitive as an object. 有些動詞必須接不定詞為受詞	agree / hope / need / want / choose / know how / would like I agreed to have an interview with him on Monday. I hope to see you again soon.
Some verbs can take either as an object. 有些動詞可以接動名詞或不定詞做為受詞	like / love / hate / prefer / try / start I'd prefer speaking / to speak with you in person. He tried calling / to call you this morning.

4 Fill in the blanks using the gerund or infinitive form of the verb given in brackets. If either can be used, write <u>both</u> forms.

1 It's OK. I don't mind _____. *(wait)*

2 I chose _____ a message rather than call again later. *(leave)*

3 Hello. I'd like _____ to John Smith, please. *(speak)*

4 I just hate _____ in sick when there's so much work to do. *(call)*

5 Sorry. I don't know how _____ calls. *(transfer)*

6 I just need _____ you on hold for a minute. *(put)*

7 I want _____ my appointment. *(reschedule)*

8 I really dislike _____ complaints. *(make)*

9 I started _____ the message, but he hung up. *(take)*

10 Let's finish _____ this problem later. *(discuss)*

Infinitives for Reasons
用不定詞表達原因

You can use an infinitive to explain why you did something.
不定詞可用以說明做某件事的原因

I'm calling . . .		to discuss our meeting.
I'm ringing . . .	**why**	to see if you have some free time later.
I called yesterday . . .		to make an appointment.
I left a message . . .		to let you know about the meeting.

5 Complete the conversations using an infinitive (to + verb).
The first conversation has been completed for you.

1 Hello. Is this hotel reception? I'm calling _____to make_____

_____a complaint_____.

My room is very dirty.

2 Hello. Is that Hetty's Hat Shop? I'm calling _____

_____. I'd like to buy three of your

most expensive hats, please.

3 Hello. Is Peter there? Hi, Peter. It's Sam. I'm just ringing

_____ to a party on Saturday.

It's my birthday.

4 Hello. I'm calling _____.

My tooth hurts, and I need to see a dentist as soon as

possible.

5 Hello, Mr. Jones? It's Sally Brown here.

I'm calling _____.

Can we meet at 3:30 instead of 2:30?

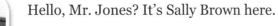

6 Pair Work! Discuss how to fill in the blanks in the following dialogues. Compare your answers with the class.

1

A   Hello. Thank you for calling Microspot Computer Company. How may I help you?

B   _____

A   Yes. I'll transfer your call. _____

2

A   Hello. James speaking.

B   _____

A   Oh, hi, Paul! _____

B   I'm _____

A   Sure. Sounds good. Call me later with the details.

B   OK. _____

A   Bye.

3

A   Hello?

B   Hello. Is this John?

A   No, _____

B   Oh, _____

7 With your partner, role-play some conversations between Bruce Grain from the Greenfield Furniture Company and one of the people below. You can use the example conversation to help you.

Example

Bruce	Hello. Greenfield Furniture Company. How may I help you?
Bob	Hello. I'd like to make a complaint. Can I talk to the manager?
Bruce	This is he. What's the problem?
Bob	I bought a chair from your company last week, but it broke when I sat on it.
Bruce	OK, sir. Let me just transfer you to our complaints department.

Bob Davies

Customer

He wants to make a complaint about something he bought from Bruce's company.

👤	**Jane Grain**	**Jenny Bond**	**Jeff Bloom**
👥	Bruce's wife	Job candidate	Friend
💬	She wants to remind Bruce to make dinner reservations for tonight.	She received a letter telling her to call and arrange an interview.	He wants to ask Bruce to go for a drink after work.

VI Now, Time to Pronounce!

Vowels (long vs. short vowels) 母音（長母音 vs. 短母音） [i] [ɪ]

8 Listen and repeat the words that you hear.

101

[i] seat   greed   sheep   see   meat

[ɪ] pin   it   ship   grit   mint

102 Listen and ⟨circle⟩ the words that you hear.

1 meat | mitt   **2** sheep | ship   **3** greet | grit   **4** weep | whip   **5** leap | lip

103 Now, listen and repeat the following sentences. Then write the <u>underlined</u> words in the correct box.

→ <u>This</u> boy likes to <u>eat</u> <u>eels</u> from the <u>sea</u>.

→ <u>We</u> never <u>sit</u> on the <u>beach</u> <u>in</u> <u>winter</u>.

[i]

[ɪ]
This

Asking for a Favor 請求協助

I. Topic Preview

1 Asking a friend for a favor 向朋友求助

> Could you do me a favor?
> Could you lend me some money?

> Sure. What is it?
> (willing) OK. How much do you need?
> (unwilling) Sorry, I'm broke.

2 Asking a stranger for a favor 向陌生人求助

> Excuse me. Could you help me with something?

> Oh, I'm sorry. I'm busy at the moment.

> It'll just take a second. I'd be ever so grateful.

> OK. What do you need?

> Could you hold my coffee for a minute?

3 Asking for permission to do something 徵求做某件事的許可

> Do you mind if I use your phone to go online?

> (willing) No, not at all.
> (unwilling) Sorry. My phone's not working.

4 Asking for something extra 額外索取某物

> Excuse me. Could I get some more ketchup?
> And could I get another coke, too?

> Sure. I'll take care of it for you right away.
> Sure. I'll be right back.

II. Vocabulary & Phrases 🎧 105

give me a lift / a ride
讓我搭便車

lend me some money 借我一點錢

lend me your umbrella 借我你的傘

help me move
幫我搬家

feed my cat
幫我餵貓

watch my stuff
幫我顧東西

pick up the check/bill for me
幫我付錢

let me use your phone
借我用你的手機

get me something from the supermarket
去超市幫我買東西

let me stay at your house
讓我住在你家

another 另一個

an extra 再一個

a couple more 再多一點

a few more 再多幾個

some more
再多一些

Sentence Patterns 🎧 106

 Asking for a favor 請求協助 (informal→formal/polite)
（非正式 → 正式／禮貌的）

Can you *lend me your umbrella*?
Could you *lend me your umbrella*?
Would you mind *lending me your umbrella*?
Would you *lend me your umbrella*?

Note
Could you **lend** *me* some money?
→ Could I *borrow* some money?
Would **you** *let me* stay at your house?
→ Could I stay at your house?

 Asking for permission 徵求許可 (informal→formal/polite)
（非正式 → 正式／禮貌的）

Can I *use your phone*?
Could I *use your phone*?
Is it OK if I *use your phone*?
Do you mind if I *use your phone*?
Would you mind if I *used your phone*?
May I *use your phone*?

Would you mind ...?

Would you mind lending me some money? 你介不介意借我一些錢？

Answer	Meaning
No, not at all.	**I'm willing to help you.**
Sure. No problem.	**I'm willing to help you.**
Yes, I would.	**I'm not willing to help you.**
Sorry, I can't.	**I'm not willing/able to help you.**

 Asking for more 索取更多物品 (informal→formal/polite)
（非正式 → 正式／禮貌的）

Can I get another *cup of coffee*?
Could I get an extra *plate*?
Is it possible for me to get a couple more *forks*?
Would it be possible for me to get some more *water*?

III. Now, Time to Listen!

1 Grace is asking her friend Paul for some favors. Try to guess what favor she is asking.
(107) Write the number of the conversation (1-5) above the correct picture.

| **1** _____ | **2** *1* _____ | **3** _____ | **4** _____ | **5** _____ |

| W U | W U | W U | W U | W U |

➡ (108) Now, listen to the complete conversations. Which of the favors is Paul willing to do? Circle willing (**W**) or unwilling (**U**) under the picture of each request.

2 Listen to the conversations and fill in the blanks. Then read the questions and check ☑ the correct answers.
(109)

1
Man	Excuse me. I'm so sorry to bother you. _____ help me with something?
Woman	Sure.
Man	I just need to go to the bathroom for a minute. Would you mind _____?
Woman	Oh, sorry. _____. I'm just about to leave.

     ⓐ This is a conversation between ☐ *two friends* ☐ *two strangers*.
     ⓑ This situation most likely happens in a ☐ *café* ☐ *classroom*.

2
Woman	Hi, James! I was wondering if you could _____.
Man	I'll do my best. What's up?
Woman	I'm moving next week. Could you maybe _____?
Man	Yeah, _____.

     ⓐ The man is ☐ *unwilling* ☐ *willing* to help the woman move house.
     ⓑ The woman probably ☐ *knows the man well* ☐ *doesn't know the man well*.

3
Man	It's raining outside. Jo, _____ if I use your phone to call a taxi?
Woman	_____. Here you go. Oh, but can you do me a favor?
Man	Sure. Anything.
Woman	Could you _____ for lunch? I only have a couple of dollars left.

     ⓐ The woman ☐ *lets* ☐ *doesn't let* the man use her phone.
     ⓑ The woman ☐ *has* ☐ *doesn't have* enough money for lunch.

IV. Now, Grammar Time!

Auxiliary verbs 助動詞：
can / could / will / would /
shall / should / may

We use these auxiliary verbs to <u>make requests</u>, <u>make offers</u>, and <u>give advice and suggestions</u>.

助動詞可以用來表達要求、提供服務或物品，以及提出建議或提議。

Informal 非正式 ⬇ Formal / Polite 正式／禮貌的	Requesting Permission 請求許可	Requesting Something/A Favor 索求物品／協助
	Can I go to the bathroom?	Can I get another piece of cake?
	Could I use your pen?	Will you open the window for me?
	Would you mind if I *sat* here?	Could you do me a favor?
	May I ask a question?	Would you mind *helping* me move?
		Would you hold this for me?

Informal 非正式 ⬇ Formal / Polite 正式／禮貌的	Offers 提供物品	Suggestions and Advice 提議和建議
	Can I get you something to drink?	You could maybe go see a doctor.
	I'll move that for you.	You should definitely go see a doctor.
	Shall I get you a chair?	John will help if you pay him.
	Would you like another cup of tea?	Sam would come if you *called* him.
	May I help you?	

③ Read the sentences and fill in the blanks with an appropriate auxiliary verb. There may be more than one correct answer. The first sentence has been completed for you.

1 Hi, Jenny. ___*Can/Could*___ I use your computer for a second?

2 Excuse me. _____ you please lower your voice? This is a library.

3 You look cold. _____ you like me to close the window?

4 Pete, _____ you come with me to the store? I need help carrying the shopping bags.

5 _____ you like some more cookies, Grandma?

6 Excuse me. _____ I take this chair?

7 Hmm. I'm not sure. Maybe you _____ send her some flowers.

8 _____ you mind giving me a ride home, Bill?

9 _____ I get you another drink, Sarah?

10 I think he _____ say yes if you ask him nicely.

4 Pair Work! Look at the pictures and complete the short dialogues using a request, an offer, or a suggestion.

a

_____
_____
_____

Sure. No problem.
You can sleep on the sofa.

b

Oh no! Was that the last piece of cake? It was so tasty.

_____
_____
There's another cake in the kitchen.

c

You look hungry. _____
_____
_____

_____
_____
_____ Thanks, Mom.

d

Hey, man. _____
_____
_____

I don't have time to go out for lunch. _____
_____
_____

Sure. What do you need?

V. Now, Time to Speak!

5 With a partner, take turns making and answering requests using the prompts below.

Example *I'm cold.*

A | Could you close the window?
B | Sure. No problem.

A | Would you mind closing the window?
B | Sorry, I'm quite hot. Can we leave it open?

Prompts

1 *I'm trying to sleep.*
2 *I'm hungry.*
3 *I'm going on vacation next week.*
4 *My car broke down.*
5 *I'm having a party.*

6 *I don't know how to send an email.*
7 *The shampoo is on the top shelf.*
8 *I lost my phone.*
9 *I'm broke.*
10 *It's raining outside.*

Requests

show me how to do something

help me reach something

lend me your coat

turn the music down

make me something to eat

help me decorate

110

Customer	Excuse me. Could I get another fork? This one fell on the floor.
Waiter	Of course. I'll take care of it right away. Do you need anything else?
Customer	Could I get some more salt, too?
Waiter	Sure. I'll be right back.

some more . . .	mustard	bread	
an extra / another	chair	cup of coffee	glass of juice
a couple / a few more . . .	spoons	pieces of cake	bowls of soup

VI. Now, Time to Pronounce!

Vowels (long vs. short vowels)　母音（長母音 vs. 短母音）　[e]　[ɛ]

7 Listen and repeat the words that you hear.

🎧 111

[e]　　locate　　dale　　late　　grave　　eight

[ɛ]　　bet　　said　　extra　　pet　　bread

8 Listen and repeat the following sentences. Write [e] or [ɛ] in the spaces given.

🎧 112　The first space has been filled in for you.

1　Please, can you wait for me to set down the plate?
　　　　　[e]　　　　　[ ]　　　　　[ ]

2　Ten raindrops hit the windowpane.
　[ ] [ ]　　　　　　　[ ]

3　Mick West failed the test eight times.
　　[ ] [ ]　　　[ ] [ ]

4　The Jets played the game very well.
　　[ ] [ ]　　[ ] [ ] [ ]

9 Listen to the words and put them in the correct box.

🎧 113　**1** spend　**2** Spain　**3** kept　**4** ballet

5 day　**6** left　**7** slept　**8** gray

[e]

[ɛ]

UNIT 10 Health Situations 健康情況

I. Topic Preview 114

1 *Expressing physical discomfort* 表達身體不適

Ooo . . . I'm not feeling too well. I feel like I'm going to be sick.

What's wrong? Sit down and drink some water.

Are you OK? You look terrible. Do you want to go and lie down?

Ooo . . . I feel really ill. Yes, I think I will.

2 *Describing your symptoms* 描述症狀

What seems to be the problem?

I have a runny nose and I'm always shivering.

OK, anything else?

I have a rash on my stomach.

3 *Finding a solution to your health problem* 找出健康問題的解決之道

Doctor, I have a really bad headache. Yes, I watch TV until late at night.

Do you watch a lot of TV? You should watch less TV.

Doctor, I can't get to sleep.

Take these sleeping pills.

4 *Calling in sick for work* 打電話請病假

I don't think I can come in to work today.

Oh, why not?

I'm feeling really ill. I have a terrible stomachache.

What did the doctor say?

He told me to stay home and rest.

82

II. Vocabulary & Phrases 〔115〕

a cold 感冒

the flu 流感

a rare disease 罕見疾病

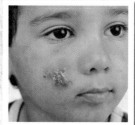
an infection 感染

measles 麻疹

a stomachache 胃痛

a runny nose 流鼻水

a fever 發燒

insomnia 失眠

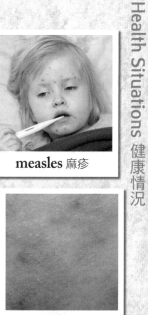
a rash 疹子

feel dizzy 頭昏

cough 咳嗽

sneeze 打噴嚏

feel nauseous
噁心;想吐

itch / scratch
發癢／抓癢

hurt 受傷

Sentence Patterns 〔116〕

- What's wrong?
  What's the matter?
  Are you OK?
  You look terrible.
  I don't feel well. / I'm not feeling too well. / I feel ill.
- I have _a runny nose_.
  I have _a_ terrible _fever_.
  I _feel dizzy_ all the time.
  My _throat_ _hurts_.
  My _eyes_ _itch_.
- Do you _feel nauseous_?
  Do you _feel dizzy_ or have _a fever_?

- I think you have _a stomach infection_.
  I think you have _the flu_.
- Do you _drink a lot of coffee_?
  Do you _watch a lot of TV_?
- You should _drink more water_.
  You should _watch less TV_.
- Rest for a few days.
  Don't _scratch it_!
  Take _these pills_.
- The doctor told me to _take this medicine_
  and _get some rest_.

1 Listen to the following conversations between a doctor and his patients. Then fill in
(117) the missing information in the table. The first column has been completed for you.

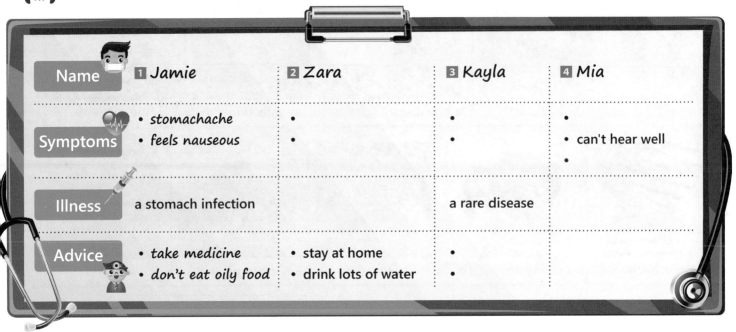

Name	① Jamie	② Zara	③ Kayla	④ Mia
Symptoms	• stomachache • feels nauseous	• •	• •	• can't hear well •
Illness	a stomach infection		a rare disease	
Advice	• take medicine • don't eat oily food	• stay at home • drink lots of water	• •	

2 Jack is calling in sick for work. Listen to his phone call and number the things below (1-5)
(118) in the order they're mentioned.

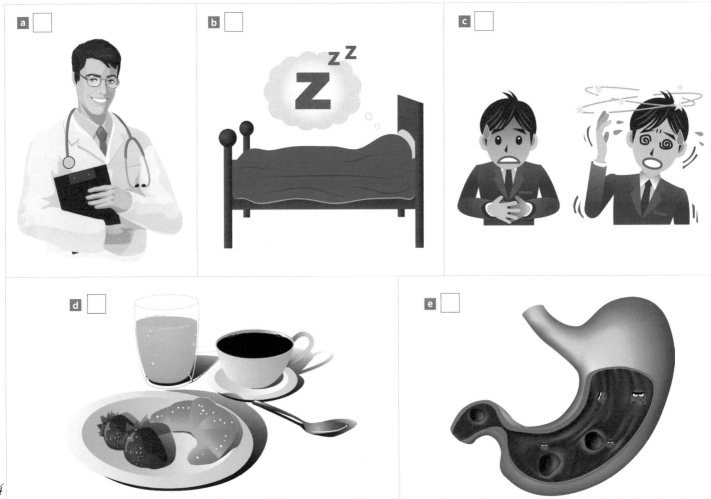

a

b

c

d

e

| eczema 濕疹 | food poisoning 食物中毒 | a sore throat 喉嚨痛 | a headache 頭痛 | the runs 拉肚子 | muscle pain 肌肉痠痛 |

More Illnesses and Symptoms 更多疾病和症狀

| apply cream 塗抹乳膏 | gargle with salt water 用鹽水漱口 | take painkillers 吃止痛藥 | take sleeping pills 服用安眠藥 | drink warm soup 喝熱湯 | apply a cold compress 冰敷 |

More Treatments and Advice 更多治療方式和建議

❸ Listen to the patients describe their health situations. Fill in the blanks and then match each description to the most appropriate response.

🎧 119

1 I have a _____, and I _____ all the time.

2 I _____ terrible _____ on my back.

3 I have a _____ and a _____ on my arms.

4 I _____, and I can't _____ anything.

5 My _____, and I have bad _____.

a Drink some warm soup and get some rest.

b Take these painkillers. They're good for all kinds of aches and pains.

c You should gargle with salt water and drink warm water.

d You should apply a cold compress to your forehead and apply this cream if you start to itch.

e Apply this cream twice a day and try to sleep on your front.

IV. Now, Grammar Time!

Auxiliary Verbs 助動詞 : do, does, did	Simple Present 簡單現在式		Simple Past 簡單過去式
	I, You, We, They	He, She, It, John, Mary . . .	I, You, We, They, He, She, It, John, Mary . . .
	do	**does**	**did**
Negative Statements 否定句	I don't have a headache.	He doesn't drink a lot of coffee.	Tina didn't take the medicine.
Yes/No Questions 是非問句	Do you have a sore throat?	Does it hurt if I touch your arm?	Did she apply the cream?
WH-Questions WH 問句	Why do they look so ill?	What does she usually eat?	When did you start to feel sick?

4 Change the following sentences into negative sentences. The first sentence has been changed for you.

1 I have a stomachache. ⟶ <u>I don't have a stomachache.</u>

2 My arm hurts. ⟶ _____

3 The rash itches. ⟶ _____

4 I took a sleeping pill last night. ⟶ _____

5 I have a rare disease. ⟶ _____

6 The doctor gave me medicine. ⟶ _____

5 Pair Work! Complete the following short dialogues with questions. Use the prompts to help you. The first dialogue has been completed for you.

1 Doctor | Hello. What's the matter?
Patient | I think I have food poisoning.
Doctor | <u>Did you eat anything strange yesterday?</u> *(eat / anything strange / yesterday)*

2 Patient | Doctor, I have a terrible headache.
Doctor | _____ *(have / a fever / too)*
Patient | Yes, I do. _____ *(think / it's / the flu)*

3 Patient | Doctor, I took some medicine, and it made me feel ill.
Doctor | _____ *(What / medicine / take)*
Patient | Just some painkillers.
Doctor | OK. _____ *(How many / take)*

4 Patient | Doctor, I need some sleeping pills.
Doctor | _____ *(Why / need / sleeping pills)*
Patient | Because I have terrible insomnia.

5 Doctor | What seems to be the problem?
Patient | I think I have measles.
Doctor | _____ *(Why / think / that)*
Patient | Because I have a rash all over my body.
Doctor | _____ *(itch)*

V. Now, Time to Speak!

6 Listen to the following conversations and practice them with a partner. Then use the pictures below to create similar conversations.

🎧120

A

Doctor	Hello, What seems to be the problem?
Patient	I have a runny nose and a sore throat.
Doctor	OK, I think you just have a cold.
Patient	What should I do?
Doctor	Drink lots of water and get some rest.

B

Jim	Hello. Boss? It's Jim.
Boss	Jim, you sound terrible. Are you OK?
Jim	No, not really. I feel really sick.
Boss	What's wrong?
Jim	I have a strange rash on my arms and legs, and I cough all the time.
Boss	What did the doctor say?
Jim	He said it's a rare disease. He told me to rest for a few days and take some medicine.
Boss	OK, Jim. Get well soon.

7 Role-play! Think of an illness and write the symptoms in the table below.

Tell your partner (the doctor) your symptoms. Can he or she guess your illness?

Example

Patient	Doctor, I have itchy eyes, and I sneeze all the time.
Doctor	Do you have a fever?
Patient	No.
Doctor	Do you have a cat?
Patient	Yes, I do.
Doctor	I think you have a cat allergy.

Illness

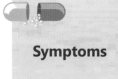

Symptoms

8 Group Work! Write an illness and its symptoms in the table below.

Then ask your classmates for their advice. Did they all give the same advice?

Example

A	Joe, I think I have the flu. I sneeze all the time. I have a fever, a sore throat, and my eyes hurt. What should I do?
B	You should go to bed and take some painkillers.

Illness and Symptoms
The flu: sneeze all the time, fever, sore throat, eyes hurt.

Name of Classmate
Joe

Advice
Go to bed.
Take painkillers.

Illness and Symptoms

_____

_____

Name of Classmate	Name of Classmate	Name of Classmate	Name of Classmate
Advice	Advice	Advice	Advice

VI. Now, Time to Pronounce!

Vowels 母音   [æ]   [ɑ]

9 Listen and repeat the words that you hear.

(121)

[æ]   cat   glass   at   sample   path

[ɑ]   arm   mart   lot   clock   spot

10 Now, listen and repeat the following sentences. Then write the <u>underlined</u> words in
(122) the correct box.

→ My <u>father</u> hit the <u>family</u> <u>cat</u> with a <u>mop</u>.

→ <u>Stop</u> <u>passing</u> under <u>palm</u> trees, <u>Matt</u>.

[æ]   [ɑ]

11 Listen to the words. Do you hear [æ] or [ɑ]? Check ☑ the box that corresponds
(123) to the sound that you hear.

[æ]   [ɑ]

1.
2.
3.
4.
5.

Talking About Sports, Talents, and Habits
談論運動、專長和嗜好

I. Topic Preview 🎧 124

1 *Talking about sporting ability* 談論運動能力

I'm really good at basketball.

Oh yeah? How good.

I can slam-dunk from the three-point line.

Wow, that's impressive!

I play on the college team, too.

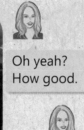

2 *Talking about sports you play regularly* 談論你固定從事的運動

Do you play any sports?

Yes, I play soccer quite often.

How often?

Oh, about once a week. You?

I don't play any sports, but I watch a lot on TV.

3 *Telling someone about your hidden talents* 將你所不為人知的專長告訴某人

I can play the violin.

I can do magic, too.

Oh really? I didn't know that!

You're full of surprises! Show me!

4 *Confessing bad habits!* 坦承你的壞習慣！

Do you have any bad habits?

Yes, but I don't want to say.

I'll tell you mine if you tell me yours.

OK. I pick my nose sometimes.

Gross! I bite my nails.

That's not too bad.

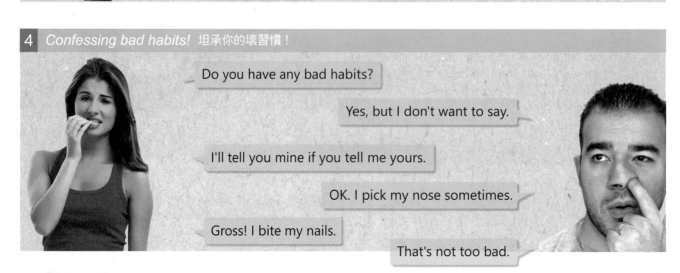

score a hat trick
完成帽子戲法

serve an ace
發出直接得分球

slam-dunk
灌籃

knock someone out
擊倒

hit a home run
擊出全壘打

play the violin
拉小提琴

do magic
變魔術

do a backflip
後空翻

make cocktails
調雞尾酒

cook a three-course meal 煮三道菜的餐點

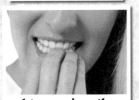

bite one's nails
咬指甲

pick one's nose
挖鼻孔

snore 打鼾

smoke 抽菸

procrastinate 拖延

Usage note

A party trick is something that you could do at a party to impress your friends, like a backflip or a card trick.
派對把戲是可以在派對上面表演，讓朋友驚艷的活動，例如後空翻或紙牌魔術。
A talent is something more special, like playing the violin or cooking well.
才能是比較特別的專長，例如拉小提琴或烹飪。

Sentence Patterns

- Are you any good at _basketball_?
  I'm pretty good.
  Are you kidding? I'm great!
- I'm really good at _tennis_. I play on the _school_ team.
- I _serve an ace_ _every time_.
- That's impressive. You're full of surprises!
- I _box_ _on a regular basis_. / I _go swimming_ _twice a week_.
- Do you have any hidden talents?
  What's your party trick?
  I can _do a backflip_.
- Oh! I didn't know you could _do magic_!
- Do you have any bad habits?
  What are your bad habits?
  I _smoke_ _sometimes_.

Frequency Adverbs 頻率副詞

★ once a <u>day</u>	一天一次
★ twice a <u>week</u>	一週兩次
★ three times a <u>month</u>	一個月三次
★ now and then	偶爾
★ without fail	必定
★ quite often	經常
★ regularly	固定
★ on a regular basis	固定
★ every time / every game	每一次／每一場比賽

Now, Time to Listen!

1 Listen to Simon and Sue talk about sports. Then check ☑ the correct box.

127

1 Sue plays  now and then.

a ☐   b ☐   c ☐

2 Sue plays with her  .

a ☐   b ☐   c ☐

3 Simon and Sue both play  .

a ☐   b ☐   c ☐

128 Now, listen to the second part of the dialogue and check ☑ the statements that are true.

a ★ ☐ Simon likes to play baseball more than hockey.

b ★ ☐ Sue watches baseball on TV.

c ★ ☐ Sue plays baseball regularly.

d ★ ☐ Simon is not very good at baseball.

e ★ ☐ Simon hits a home run every game.

f ★ ☐ Sue is not impressed by Simon's ability.

2 Diana is asking her friend Matt for help finding someone to perform at her party. Listen to their conversation and write the person's name under his or her talent.

129

a    b    c    d

_____   _____   _____   _____

92

130 Listen to the dialogue again. Listen for the statements on the left, and then fill in the blanks in the replies.

1 Can you do magic?

Sorry, Diana. I can't. I can _____, though.

2 I'm going to cook a three-course meal.

Oh, I didn't _____ cook.

3 I can play the piano, too.

Well, you are _____.

4 He can saw a person in half.

Wow! That's _____.

3 Listen to the people describe their bad habits. Check ☑ the correct boxes in the table.

131

	a	b	c	d	e
1 Jerry			✔		
2 Val					
3 Emily					
4 Harry					
5 Tina					

132 Now, listen again. Take notes on how often each person performs his/her bad habits and answer the questions below.

1 Who smokes more than one cigarette a day? How many cigarettes does this person smoke a day?

_____ ⏱ ☐ **a** 20 cigarettes a day ☐ **b** 40 cigarettes a day

2 Who procrastinates most often? How often does he/she procrastinate?

_____ ⏱ ☐ **a** 10 times a day ☐ **b** five times a day

3 Who bites his or her nails most often? How often does he/she bite his/her nails?

_____ ⏱ ☐ **a** three times an hour ☐ **b** once an hour

4 Who snores more than once a week? Does he/she snore regularly?

_____ ⏱ ☐ **a** Yes, every night. ☐ **b** Yes, a few times a week.

5 Who picks his or her nose regularly? How often does he/she pick his/her nose?

_____ ⏱ ☐ **a** once an hour ☐ **b** once every couple of hours

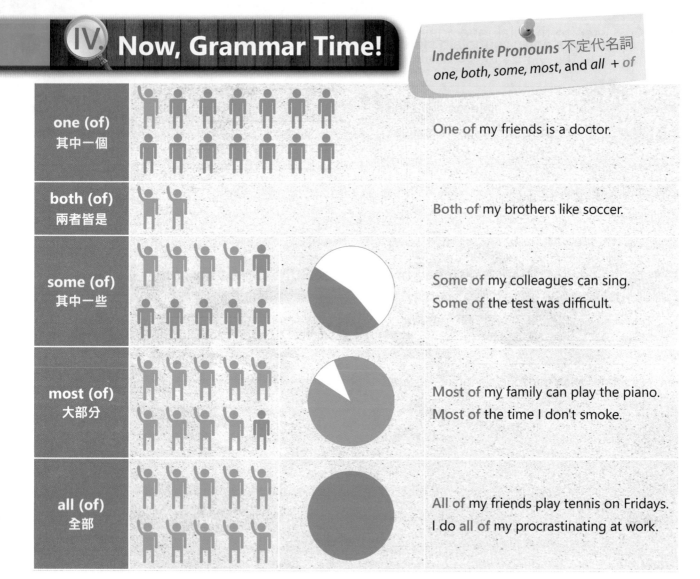

one (of) 其中一個		One of my friends is a doctor.
both (of) 兩者皆是		Both of my brothers like soccer.
some (of) 其中一些		Some of my colleagues can sing. Some of the test was difficult.
most (of) 大部分		Most of my family can play the piano. Most of the time I don't smoke.
all (of) 全部		All of my friends play tennis on Fridays. I do all of my procrastinating at work.

4 Change the following sentences into sentences that use an indefinite pronoun. The first sentence has been changed for you.

1 My friends are John, Sue, and Ian. Ian can do a backflip.

One of my friends can do a backflip.

2 I have seven colleagues. Six of them love baseball.

_____

3 My sisters are Joan and Jen. Joan can cook. Jen can cook, too.

_____

4 I have eight friends. Three of them bite their nails.

_____

5 James, John, and Jim are my bothers. James snores, John snores, and Jim snores.

_____

94

❺ Look at the diagram showing the people Bill knows. Then fill in the blanks with indefinite pronouns.

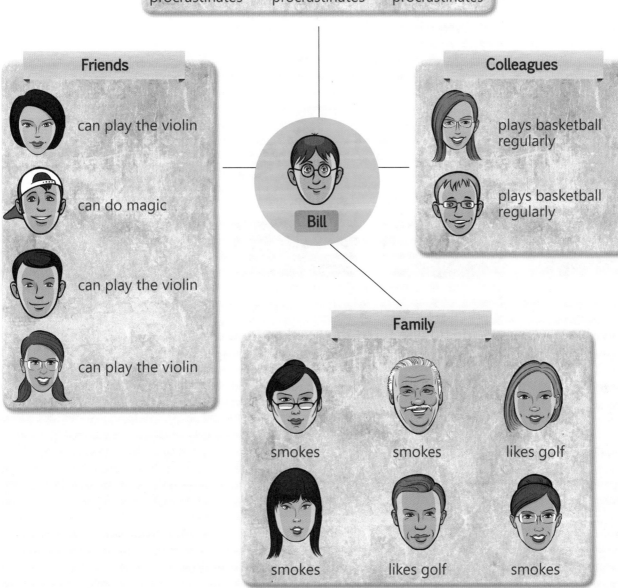

1 _____One of_____	Bill's friends can do magic.
2 _____	Bill's friends can play the violin.
3 _____	Bill's classmates procrastinate.
4 _____	Bill's family smoke.
5 _____	Bill's family like golf.
6 _____	Bill's colleagues play basketball regularly.

6 Pair Work! Listen to the dialogue, and then practice it with your partner.

A	Do you play any sports regularly?
B	Yeah, I really like to play American football.
A	How often do you play?
B	I play about three times a week with my classmates. I'm on the school team.
A	Are you any good?
B	Are you kidding me? I score a touchdown every game.
A	Wow! That's pretty impressive.

➡ Now, tell your partner about your own sporting abilities and habits. You can use the pictures to help you.

hit a hole in one
一竿進洞

bowl a strike
打出全倒

score a touchdown
觸地得分

catch a wave
追浪

pot the black
打進黑球

7 With a partner, decide how to fill in the blanks in the dialogue. Discuss your answers with the class. Then practice the dialogue with your partner.

Peter	Do you have any hidden talents, Sandy?
Sandy	_____.
Peter	Really? I never knew that! When did you learn how to _____?
Sandy	I learned _____.
	_____ taught me.
Peter	And how often do you do it now?
Sandy	Now? _____.
	I usually _____.
Peter	I see. How about party tricks? Do you have one of those?
Sandy	Well, I can _____, but that's all. It's not very impressive. What's yours?
Peter	I can _____.
Sandy	_____! I wish I could do that!

➡ Now, have a similar conversation with your partner. Tell the class about your partner's talents or party tricks.

More talents and party tricks:

dance 跳舞
juggle 雜耍

draw caricatures 畫漫畫

do impressions 模仿

bake 烘焙

8 Look at the pictures and discuss them with your partner. Where are the people in the photos? Are they talking about bad habits, sporting ability, or talents?

1

2

3

➡ Now, choose one photo and create a short dialogue. Use the sentences below to help you start.

A : *Did you know that I'm amazing at basketball?*

A : *What talent are you going to perform today?*

A : *My husband has a really bad habit.*

Ⓥ Now, Time to Pronounce!

Vowels (long vs. short vowels) 母音（長母音 vs. 短母音） [o] [ɔ]

9 Listen and repeat the words that you hear.

(134)
[o] boat   toe   hello   grow   over

[ɔ] law   all   dawn   always   hall

(135) ➡ Now, try saying the following words aloud. Then listen and check your pronunciation. The sound has been <u>underlined</u> for you.

[o] c<u>oa</u>t n<u>o</u> s<u>oa</u>p r<u>o</u>ll f<u>o</u>ld   [ɔ] st<u>a</u>lk j<u>aw</u> l<u>aw</u>n <u>a</u>lways h<u>a</u>ll

10 Listen to the sentences. Then read them aloud and ⌐circle⌐ all the words that contain
(136) the [o] sound.

I told you not to walk in the old moat.
The bold fawn crawled past the yawning toad.

(137) ➡ Now, read the sentences again and <u>underline</u> the words that contain the [ɔ] sound.

Finding an Apartment 找房子

I. Topic Preview (138)

1 Calling a landlord about a new apartment 打電話給房東詢問房屋事宜

Hello. I'm calling about the apartment. Is it still available?

Hello. I'm calling about the ad that was in today's paper.

Hello. I saw your notice about an apartment for rent.

2 Asking questions about the apartment 詢問租屋相關問題

 Where is it exactly?

 It's on Newton Road, number five.

 Your ad says it's a one-bedroom apartment.

 Yes, that's right.

 How many rooms are there altogether?

 Altogether, there are four rooms.

Is it furnished?

No, it's unfurnished.

And how much is the rent?

It's $1,500 a month.

Are utilities included in the rent?

Water is included, but not electricity or gas.

3 Living with a roommate and making house rules 與室友同住並制訂居家規範

We should take turns cleaning the apartment.

We should keep air conditioner use to a minimum.

We should split the bills 50-50.

We should check with each other before inviting friends over.

II. Vocabulary & Phrases

rent 房租

furnished apartment 附家具的公寓

unfurnished apartment 未附家具的公寓

utilities 水電設施

neighborhood 鄰近地區

communal/private laundry facilities 公用／私人洗衣設備

double bed 雙人床

refrigerator 冰箱

air conditioning 空調設備

central heating 暖氣

subway station 地鐵站

dining room 餐廳

bedroom 臥室

living room 客廳

kitchen 廚房

bathroom 浴室

balcony 陽台

 Common Types of Apartments 常見的公寓型態

A studio apartment: a small, cheap apartment. There are usually only two rooms—a bathroom and a combined sleeping and living area.
套房：小型、便宜的公寓，通常只有兩個房間——一間浴室和一間結合睡覺與起居空間的房間。

A one or two-bedroom apartment: bigger apartments with other rooms separate from the bedrooms.
單房或雙房公寓：空間較大，除了臥室之外還會有其他房間。

Sentence Patterns

- Hello. I'm calling about the apartment. Is it still available?
- Where is it exactly? / What's the address?
- How many _rooms_ are there? / Your ad says it's a _two-bedroom_ apartment.
- Is there a _kitchen_? / Is it _furnished_? / What's the _neighborhood_ like? / Is there _a subway station_ close by?
- How much is the rent?
  It's _$1,600_ a month.
- Are utilities included?
  Water is included, but _gas_ and _electricity_ aren't.
- We should _split the rent 60-40_. We should _take turns cleaning the bathroom_.

III. Now, Time to Listen!

1 Listen to Jake call two different landlords. Fill in the blanks in the notes that he makes.

141

A

Address? ➡ _____ Watt Street

Neighborhood? ➡ very lively, lots of _____, close to _____

Rent? ➡ $_____ a month

Utilities? ➡ _____ and _____ included in rent

Rooms? ➡ bathroom, bedroom, _____, _____

Furnished? ➡ partly – _____ and a double bed

Other? ➡ air-conditioning, _____, _____ laundry facilities

B

Address? ➡ 60 Hawking _____

Neighborhood? ➡ very _____, mostly other _____ buildings

Rent? ➡ $_____ a month

Utilities? ➡ _____ in the rent

Rooms? ➡ _____, _____/living room combined

Furnished? ➡ fully – _____, closet, desk, _____

Other? ➡ _____ with _____ laundry facilities

2 Earlier in the day, Jake spoke to his girlfriend about what kind of apartment they'd like to rent. Listen to their conversation and check ☑ the things his girlfriend wants.

142

a ☐ A kitchen	**g** ☐ Close to a subway station
b ☐ A balcony	**h** ☐ Communal laundry facilities
c ☐ Rent < $1,300	**i** ☐ Private laundry facilities
d ☐ Rent > $1,300	**j** ☐ Furnished
e ☐ A lively neighborhood	**k** ☐ Unfurnished
f ☐ A quiet neighborhood	

➡ Based on what you've heard, check ☑ the apartment that you think best suits Jake and his girlfriend.

Apartment: ☐ A   ☐ B

❸ Listen to these conversations between new roommates. Match each conversation to the picture that best illustrates it. Then write down the house rule they decide on.

Common House Rules

- keep something clean 維持某物清潔

- take turns doing something 輪流做某事

- split something 50-50 / 60-40
  五五／六四分攤某事

- check with each other before doing something
  做某事之前與對方商量

- keep something to a minimum
  做某事的頻率降到最低

a

b

c d

e

RULES

1	e	take turns taking out the trash
2		
3		
4		
5		

IV. Now, Grammar Time!

Indefinite Pronouns
不定代名詞

$\left\{\begin{array}{l}\text{a few}\\\text{a little}\\\text{many}\\\text{much}\end{array}\right. + \textit{of}$

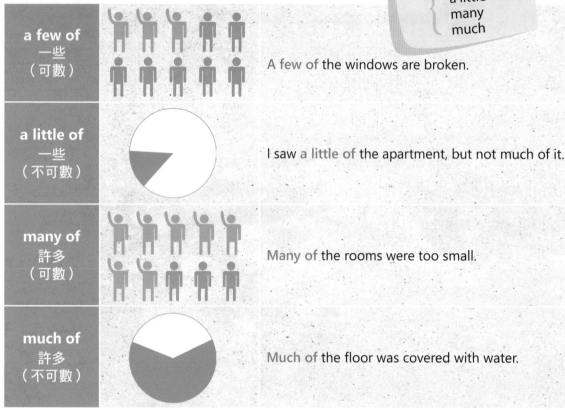

a few of 一些 （可數）		A few of the windows are broken.
a little of 一些 （不可數）		I saw a little of the apartment, but not much of it.
many of 許多 （可數）		Many of the rooms were too small.
much of 許多 （不可數）		Much of the floor was covered with water.

4 Change the following sentences into sentences that use indefinite pronouns. The first sentence has been changed for you.

1 Seventy percent of the time, I take out the trash.

<u>Much of the time</u>, I take out the trash.

2 I saw 10 apartments last week. Three looked quite nice.

_____ I saw last week looked quite nice.

3 Last year I had seven problems with my apartment. My landlord helped me solve five of them.

My landlord helped me solve _____ with my apartment last year.

4 I clean 20% of the apartment each week.

I clean _____ each week.

5 I pay 80% of the rent.

I pay _____.

V. Now, Time to Speak!

5 Pair Work! Discuss how to complete the following conversations. Compare your answers with the class.

1

Caller	Hello. I'm calling about the apartment. _____ _____
Landlord	Yes, it's still available. Would you like to come and see it?
Caller	Maybe. _____ _____
Landlord	Sure. Ask away.
Caller	The ad says it's a two-bedroom apartment. _____ _____
Landlord	There are five rooms altogether: two bedrooms, _____ _____.

2

Caller	_____
Landlord	_____ There's a refrigerator, beds, and closets, but no tables or chairs.
Caller	_____
Landlord	The rent is $2,500 a month.
Caller	Are utilities included in that?
Landlord	_____, but not electricity.
Caller	_____
Landlord	It's very lively. There are lots of _____ nearby.
Caller	OK. Can I come round to see it this afternoon?
Landlord	Sure. Come round any time after 2:00 p.m.

➡ What other questions could the caller ask the landlord? Discuss with your partner and share your ideas with the class.

6 Role-play! Create dialogues using the pictures and Exercise **5** to help you. Alternate your roles as landlord and caller.

7 Imagine you and your partner are roommates. Look at the following situations and suggest rules that might solve the problems.

Example Your roommate never washes the dishes.

*"We should **take turns washing the dishes. I'll do them on Mondays ...**"*

1 Your roommate uses more electricity than you. You don't want to pay half of the electricity bill.

2 The living room is really dirty. You need to do something about it.

3 Whenever you want to watch TV, your roommate always wants to watch a different show.

4 Your roommate smokes in the apartment. You hate the smell.

5 Your roommate always leaves a lot of hair in the bath.

6 Your roommate loves to sing loudly in the living room while you're trying to read.

Now, Time to Pronounce!

Vowels (long vs. short vowels)　母音（長母音 vs. 短母音）　[u]　[ʊ]

8 Listen and repeat the words that you hear.

144

[u]　　clue　　threw　　glue　　new　　true

[ʊ]　　foot　　pull　　hood　　book　　should

145 　　Now, listen to the following sentences. Then read them aloud and write the underlined words in the correct box.

→ Would you please put those two lights out?

→ The bluebirds flew far from the woods to drink in the brook.

[u]　　　　　　　[ʊ]

9 Listen to the words. Do you hear [u] or [ʊ]? Check ☑ the box that corresponds to 146 the sound that you hear.

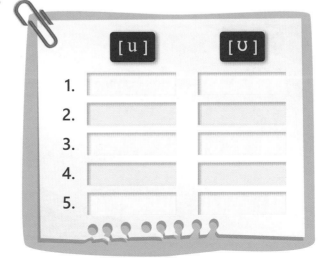

	[u]	[ʊ]
1.		
2.		
3.		
4.		
5.		

105

Talking About Traffic and Transportation
談論交通與交通方式

I. Topic Preview 🎧147

---

1 *Calling a cab/taxi* 叫計程車

Hello. Super Cab.
  Sure. When would you like your pickup?
Can I have your last name, please?

Hello. Could I order a cab from the Seaview Hotel to the train station, please?
  Tomorrow morning at 9:00 a.m.
Jones.

---

2 *Discussing the fare* 討論車資

That'll be $18, please.
There's an extra charge of two dollars after 10:00 p.m.

But the meter says $16.
Here's $20. Keep the change.

---

3 *Buying a bus/train/subway ticket* 購買公車／火車／地鐵票

Could I get a one-way ticket to Jamestown, please?

Sure. That'll be $2.50.

How much is a one-day pass?
Until when is it valid?

A one-day pass is $8.50.
It's valid until 4:30 a.m. tomorrow morning.

---

4 *Asking for travel information* 詢問交通資訊

Which bus should I take?

Take the number 35 bus.

Where should I get off?

Get off at the third stop.

How long will the journey take?

It'll take about an hour.

II. Vocabulary & Phrases 🎧148

 cab/taxi 計程車

 train 火車

 bus 公車

 subway/tube/metro 地鐵；捷運

 one-day pass 一日券

 weekly pass 一週券

 monthly pass 月票

 fare 車資

 meter 計費表

automatic ticket machine 自動售票機

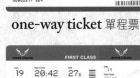 one-way ticket 單程票

return ticket 來回票

 train station 火車站

 taxi stand 計程車招呼站

bus stop 公車站

platform 月台

 route map 路線圖

Sentence Patterns 🎧149

- Could I order a cab from *the train station* to *the Royal Hotel please*?
- When would you like your pickup?
  This afternoon at *5:00 p.m.*
- That'll be *$13*.
  But the meter says *$10*.
  There's an extra charge.
  Here's *$15*. Keep the change.
- Could I get a *return ticket* to *Petersville*, please?
- How much is a *monthly pass*?
- Until when is it valid? / When does it expire?
  It's valid until *the 27th of this month*.
- Can I buy *tickets* here? / Where can I buy *a route map*?

- Which bus should I take?
  Take the *bus* that's going to *Newcastle*.
  Take bus number *432*.
- Where do I board the *train to Newtown*?
  Which *platform* does the *train to Newtown* leave from?
  At/From *platform four*.
- Where should I get off?
  Which stop should I get off at?
  Get off at *Stevenson Station*.
  Get off at the *fourth* stop.
- How long will the journey take?
  About *two hours*.

1 Rob is ordering a taxi. Today's date is Monday, October 17. Listen to Rob's phone call
(150) and fill in as much of the taxi receipt as you can.

Taxi Receipt

★ Super Cab ★

Date	_____	Pickup Time	_____
Customer	Mr. _____		
From	Newtown Central _____		
To	_____ on Fifth Street		

(151) ➡ Now, listen to Rob getting out of the taxi. Fill in the rest of the receipt.

Fare	$ _____
Amount Paid	$ _____
Change	$ _____

TAXI

2 Listen to the customer try to buy a train ticket. Then check ☑ the correct answers.

(152) **1** What kind of ticket does the customer ask for first?

- ☐ **a** a return ticket from Newtown to Oldport
- ☐ **b** a one-way ticket to Oldport
- ☐ **c** a return ticket from Oldport to Newtown

2 What kind of ticket does the customer buy in the end?

- ☐ **a** a one-day pass
- ☐ **b** a monthly pass
- ☐ **c** a weekly pass

3 Based on the information you heard, what is today's date?

- ☐ **a** the 16th
- ☐ **b** the 10th
- ☐ **c** the first

4 With his new pass, which of the following routes can the customer NOT travel?

- ☐ **a** Newtown to Oldport
- ☐ **b** Oldport to Newtown
- ☐ **c** Newtown to Swanbrook

❸ Listen to the travelers ask for information. Check ☑ the information that's given to each traveler.

153

1 a   Here!   b   Here!

2 a   b

3 a   Platform 4 →   b   Platform 2 →

4 a   02:00-03:00 p.m.   b   02:00-05:00 p.m.

5 a   Kaohsiung   b   Taipei

IV. Now, Grammar Time!

Active and Passive Voice
主動與被動語態
for modal auxiliary verbs
(can, must, should etc.)
情態助動詞 can、must、should 等

Active Voice 主動語態 focusing on the *doer* of the verb 強調動作的「執行者」	Passive Voice 被動語態 focusing on the *receiver* of the verb 強調動作的「接受者」
You can **buy** tickets at the ticket counter. You must **use** this ticket before midnight tonight.	Tickets can **be bought** at the ticket counter. This ticket must **be used** before midnight tonight.

Note To form the passive voice you need to use the **past participle** of the verb.
必須使用動詞的過去分詞來構成被動語態。

Past Participles 過去分詞

Regular Verbs 規則動詞	Base Form 原形	Simple Past 過去式	Past Participle 過去分詞
	use	used	used
	board	boarded	boarded

Irregular Verbs 不規則動詞	Base Form 原形	Simple Past 過去式	Past Participle 過去分詞
	find	found	found
	buy	bought	bought
	pay	paid	paid
	take	took	taken

❹ **Change the following sentences from the active voice to the passive voice.**

1　You can find taxis at the taxi stand outside.

　　Taxis _____.

2　You can pay for monthly passes by credit card.

　　Monthly passes _____.

3　You can take a train to Oldport from Newtown Central Station.

　　Trains to Oldport _____.

4　You must use your return ticket on the day you buy it.

　　Your return ticket _____.

5　You can board the bus to Newtown at bus stop number nine.

　　The bus to Newtown _____.

❺ Pair Work! Look at the pictures and complete the short dialogues using sentences in the passive voice.

More Travel Information 更多旅遊資訊

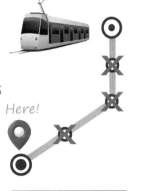

peak time 尖峰時刻	off-peak time 離峰時刻	information desk 服務台	direct/express train 直達車／快車	bus/train timetable 公車／火車時刻表

1

Excuse me.
Where can I find a route map?

Route maps _____ _____ the information desk.

2

When can I use this off-peak ticket?

🚆 **National Rail** *Peak Times*
Peak Time: 6:30-9:30 a.m.
4:30-7:30 p.m.

Off-peak tickets _____ not _____ between 6:30 and 9:30 a.m. or _____ _____

3

Hi. Can I take a direct train to London from this station?

No, but direct trains to London _____ _____ Central Station.

4

Excuse me.
Can I buy a bus ticket here?

No. Bus tickets _____ only _____ on the bus.

V. Now, Time to Speak!

6 Role-play! Use the upper halves of the taxi receipts to order a taxi. Student A should play the taxi company. Student B should play the caller. Switch roles for each receipt.

 Today's date is Monday, October 17.

Student A	Hello. Happy Cab.
Student B	Hello. I'd like to order a taxi from <u>Sunrise Hotel</u> to <u>Teatown Bus Station</u>.
Student A	No problem. When would you like your pickup?
Student B	<u>This Wednesday at 10:00 a.m.</u>
Student A	Can I have your last name, please?
Student B	Yes. It's <u>Jones, J-O-N-E-S</u>.
Student A	OK, <u>Ms. Jones</u>. Your taxi will be <u>at the Sunrise Hotel</u> waiting for you.

Taxi Receipt

Date	10/17	Pickup Time	10:30 p.m.
Customer		Mr. Smith	
From	Deelish Restaurant		
To	13 Harold Road		
Fare	$20 + $2 (10% extra charge after 10:00 p.m.)		
Amount Paid		$25	
Change		$1	

Taxi Receipt

Date	10/19	Pickup Time	10:00 p.m.
Customer		Ms. Jones	
From	Sunrise Hotel		
To	Teatown Bus Station		
Fare		$13	
Amount Paid		$15	
Change		$0	

Taxi Receipt

Date	10/17	Pickup Time	6:00 p.m.
Customer		Mr. Crooks	
From	24 William Street		
To	Oldport Airport		
Fare	$30 + $1.50 (extra charge for helping with bags)		
Amount Paid		$35	
Change		$0	

Taxi Receipt

Date	10/18	Pickup Time	2:00 p.m.
Customer		Miss Scott	
From	10 Notting Hill Drive		
To	Grantville Central Train Station		
Fare		$45	
Amount Paid		$50	
Change		$5	

Now, use the lower halves marked in yellow to pay for your journey.
Student A should play the taxi driver. Student B should play the customer.
Switch roles for each receipt.

Student A	Here we are at the <u>Teatown Bus Station</u>. That'll be <u>$13</u>, please.
Student B	Here's <u>$15</u>.
Student A	Thank you very much. Let me just get you your change.
Student B	It's OK. Keep the change.
Student A	Oh, thank you very much, sir. Here's your receipt.
Student B	Thanks. Bye.

7 Listen to the following conversation and practice it with a partner.
Then look at the tickets and create similar conversations.

(154)

Customer	Could I get a one-way ticket to Chicago, please?
Ticket seller	Sure. That'll be $18.50.
Customer	When does it expire?
Ticket seller	It's valid only for today.
Customer	And at what times can I use it?
Ticket seller	Off-peak tickets can only be used between 9:30 a.m. and 4:30 p.m. or anytime after 7:30 p.m.

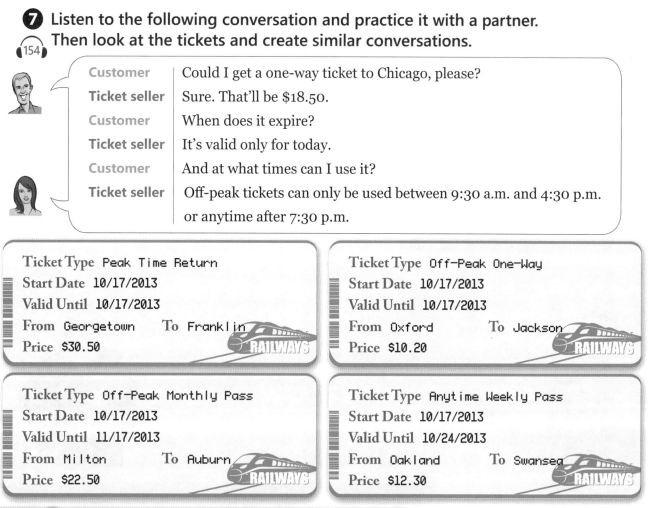

Ticket Type Peak Time Return
Start Date 10/17/2013
Valid Until 10/17/2013
From Georgetown   To Franklin
Price $30.50
RAILWAYS

Ticket Type Off-Peak One-Way
Start Date 10/17/2013
Valid Until 10/17/2013
From Oxford   To Jackson
Price $10.20
RAILWAYS

Ticket Type Off-Peak Monthly Pass
Start Date 10/17/2013
Valid Until 11/17/2013
From Milton   To Auburn
Price $22.50
RAILWAYS

Ticket Type Anytime Weekly Pass
Start Date 10/17/2013
Valid Until 10/24/2013
From Oakland   To Swansea
Price $12.30
RAILWAYS

VI Now, Time to Pronounce!

Vowels (stressed vs. unstressed vowels)
母音（重母音 vs. 輕母音）

[ʌ] [ə]

Pay attention 注意

[ʌ] and [ə] sound pretty much the same. So, how do you tell the difference?
[ʌ] 和 [ə] 的發音幾乎一模一樣，要怎麼分辨使用時機呢？

[ʌ] → stressed syllables
在重音音節使用
[ə] → unstressed syllables
在非重音音節使用

8 Listen and repeat the words that you hear.

(155)

[ʌ]   under   run   flood   gutter   done

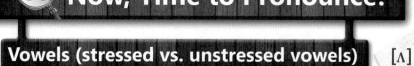

[ə]   about   balloon   cobra   asleep   alone

9 Listen and repeat the following sentences. Then (circle) all the words that contain

(156) the [ʌ] sound.

My son was taken to the funfair by his mother.

The zebra was surprised to be stuck in the mud.

(157) ➥ Now, read them again and underline all the words that contain the [ə] sound.

10 Listen to the words. Then write the correct phonetic symbol—[ʌ] or [ə]—underneath.

(158)

1	**2**	**3**	**4**	**5**	**6**	**7**	**8**
upstairs	club	chocolate	terrible	blood	above	gun	runny
[ ]	[ ]	[ ]	[ ]	[ ]	[ ]	[ ]	[ ]

I. Topic Preview (159)

1 Talking about what you do and where you work 談論工作與工作地點

What do you do for a living?

I'm a lawyer.

Which company do you work for?

I work for East Asia Law.

Is it a big company?

Yes, it's the biggest law firm in Tokyo.

2 Talking about your work hours and salary 談論工時與薪資

What hours do you work?

I usually work nine to five, but I sometimes work overtime.

I work shifts, so I often work weekends and nights.

What's your salary?
I hope you don't mind me asking.

I earn around $40,000 a year.

I get paid $10 an hour.

3 Talking about the good and bad aspects of your work 談論工作的優缺點

So, what do you like about your job?
Is there anything you hate about your job?

I get a lot of paid vacation days, which is good.
Yes, I hate my boss. He's the worst thing about my job.

4 Talking about why you left your old job 談論前一份工作的離職原因

Why did you leave your old job?

I got fired for turning up late too often.

I wanted to try something different.

II. Vocabulary & Phrases  160

law firm
法律事務所

publishing company
出版社

bank
銀行

convenience store
便利商店

café
咖啡館

salary
薪資

shift work
輪班制

full-time job
全職工作

part-time job
兼職工作

**vacation/personal/
sick days**
休假／事假／病假

minimum wage
最低工資

Christmas bonus
耶誕獎金

**(work) regular
office hours**
固定上班時間

recruitment agency
人力仲介

(work) overtime 加班

quit 辭職

be fired
被開除

Sentence Patterns 161

- What do you do for a living?
  I'm an _editor_.
- Which company do you work for?
  I work for _Oxbridge University Press_.
- Where do you work?
  I work at _a convenience store_.
- What hours do you work?
  I work _regular office hours_. / I do _shift work_. /
  I work _part-time_.

- What's your salary?
  I earn about _$35,000_ _a year_. /
  I get paid _minimum wage_.
- What do you like about your job?
  I get a lot of paid _personal days_. /
  I get a big _Christmas bonus_.
- Is there anything you hate about your job?
  The overtime is the worst thing about my job.
- Why did you leave your old job?
  I quit because I _wanted a bigger salary_.

III. Now, Time to Listen!

1 Listen to the people talk about their jobs. Then match each statement with one of the personal profiles below.

(162)

1 _____ **2** _____ **3** _____ **4** _____

---

a
Stewart Davies

Occupation: Bank manager
Working Hours: 8:00 a.m. – 6:00 p.m.
Salary: $60,000/year
Other: Often works overtime; excellent Christmas bonus

b
Alan Lee

Occupation: Convenience store clerk
Working Hours: 11:00 p.m. – 7:00 a.m.
Salary: $7.25/hour
Other: Works part-time

c
Jimmy Cooper

Occupation: Banker
Working Hours: 9:00 a.m. – 6:00 p.m.
Salary: $40,000/year
Other: Gets a lot of paid sick days and personal days.

d
Josie Burke

Occupation: Teacher
Working Hours: 8:30 a.m. – 4:00 p.m.
Salary: $40,000/year
Other: Gets a lot of paid vacation days

e
Kathy Long

Occupation: Lawyer
Working Hours: 9:00 a.m. – 8:00 p.m.
Salary: $70,000/year
Other: Often works overtime

f
Emma Carr

Occupation: Coffee maker
Working Hours: 7:30 a.m. – 3.30 p.m.
Salary: $10/hour
Other: Works part-time; gets a few paid sick days

---

(163) Listen again and fill in the blanks.

1 I work for Capital Bank. I work _____ hours, and I get a good _____ of $_____ a _____. I also get a lot of paid _____ days and _____ days, so it's actually a pretty good deal.

2 I _____ Mondays , Wednesdays, and Fridays in a _____. I do the 7:30 to 3:30 _____, and I get paid _____. I get a few paid sick days, which isn't too bad for this kind of work.

3 I work the _____ shift at 7-11. I get paid _____, and I only work on weekends. It's just a _____ for while I'm studying.

4 The _____ thing about my job is the _____ days! I get a lot of _____ vacation days each year. I get a good salary, too—around $40,000 a year. And I finish work quite _____.

116

2 Julia is looking for a new job. Use the information you hear to fill in the recruitment agency's questionnaire.

164

***A*-corn Recruitment**

Application Questionnaire

Name: _Julia Fielding_

1 What kind of work would you like?

○ **a** office work   ○ **b** shift work

2 How many hours a week would you like to work?

○ **a** 10-29   ○ **b** 30-48

3 What kind of yearly salary would you like to receive?

○ **a** $5,000 – $14,000 ○ **b** $15,000 – $30,000

○ **c** $31,000 – $45,000 ○ **d** $46,000+

4 Why did you leave your former job?

○ **a** fired   ○ **b** career change

○ **c** salary   ○ **d** work environment   ○ **e** work hours

5 What did you like most about your former job?

○ **a** colleagues   ○ **b** boss

○ **c** duties   ○ **d** work hours   ○ **e** benefits (vacation days, etc.)

6 What did you dislike most about your former job?

○ **a** colleagues   ○ **b** boss

○ **c** duties   ○ **d** work hours   ○ **e** benefits (vacation days, etc.)

Ⅳ. Now, Grammar Time!

Question Tags
附加問句

Used for checking/ confirming information you're not sure about
用來檢查／確認 你不確定的資訊

Statement 陳述句	Question Tag 附加問句
You're a lawyer,	aren't you?
You aren't a teacher,	are you?
He isn't a banker,	is he?
She was fired,	wasn't she?
Joe works regular office hours,	doesn't he?
Kathy doesn't like her boss,	does she?
Jimmy hated working here,	didn't he?

Pay attention to your intonation.

I'm right, aren't I? *You're quite sure.*

I'm right, aren't I? *You're not very sure.*

❸ Make statements with question tags using the prompts. The first question has been written for you.

1 You want to confirm that John is an engineer.

→ *John's an engineer, isn't he?*_____

2 You want to confirm that Peter works shifts.

→ _____

3 You want to check that Mark's a teacher.

→ _____

4 You want to confirm that Mike earns $20,000 a year.

→ _____

5 You want to check that Peter gets paid sick days.

→ _____

❹ Match the statements below to the correct question tags.

1 You work at the Stardust Café, •

2 Jenny works the night shift, •

3 Kenny got fired, •

4 Rose isn't a secretary, •

5 Derek can work overtime tonight, •

• **a** didn't he

• **b** doesn't she?

• **c** can't he?

• **d** is she?

• **e** don't you?

V. Now, Time to Speak!

5 Pair Work! Choose one of the jobs below. Your partner must then ask you questions and try to guess which job you chose. Use question tags to ask the questions.

Example

A	You work regular office hours, don't you?
B	No, I don't.
A	Oh, but . . . you get a lot of vacation days, don't you?
B	Yes, I do.
A	And you work in a school, don't you?
B	Yes, I do.
A	You're a teacher, aren't you?
B	Yes, I am!

bartender
酒保

accountant
會計

bank manager
銀行經理

reporter
記者

taxi driver
計程車司機

computer programmer
電腦程式工程師

surgeon
外科醫生

librarian
圖書館員

6 With your partner, choose one of the pictures. Make a list of the things you think the people like and dislike about their jobs. Then share your ideas with the class.

Some useful phrases you may need:

— the stress

— the sense of achievement

— the long hours

— meeting new people

— working with a team

— the fresh air

7 Role-play! Student A should play a recruiter for a recruitment agency. Student B should play the applicant. At the end of the interview, suggest a job to Student B.

Job Interview Questions

Student A (the recruiter)—Ask the following questions.
Student B (the applicant)—Use these models to help you answer.

What kind of work would you like?
I'd like _____ work.
How many hours a week would you like to work?
I'd like to work _____ hours a week.
What kind of yearly salary would you like to receive?
I'd like around / at least _____ a year.
Why did you leave your former job?
I left because _____.
What did you like most about your former job?
_____ was the best thing about my last job.
What did you dislike most about your former job?
I didn't like the _____ at my last job.

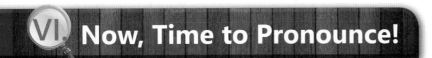

VI. Now, Time to Pronounce!

Vowels (stressed vs. unstressed vowels)
母音（重母音 vs. 輕母音）

[ɝ] [ɚ]

8 Listen and repeat the words that you hear.

165

[ɝ]　　bird　earth　fur　hurt　burn

[ɚ]　　other　winner　water　yesterday　figures

Pay attention 注意

[ɝ] and [ɚ] sound pretty much the same. So, how do you tell the difference?
[ɝ] 和 [ɚ] 的發音幾乎一模一樣，要怎麼分辨使用時機呢？

[ɝ] → stressed syllables
　　　在重音音節使用
[ɚ] → unstressed syllables
　　　在非重音音節使用

166 ➡ Now, listen to the following sentences. Then read them aloud and write the underlined words in the correct box.

➡ The <u>farmer</u> <u>heard</u> the <u>church</u> bells <u>first</u>.

➡ I got a <u>number</u> of <u>dollars</u> for good <u>work</u>.

[ɝ]　　　　　　　　　[ɚ]

- - - - - - - - - - -　　　- - - - - - - - - - -

- - - - - - - - - - -　　　- - - - - - - - - - -

- - - - - - - - - - -　　　- - - - - - - - - - -

- - - - - - - - - - -　　　- - - - - - - - - - -

9 Listen to the words. Do you hear [ɝ] or [ɚ]? Check ☑ the box that corresponds
167 to the sound you hear.

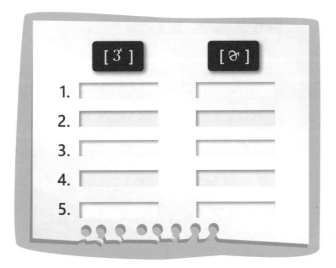

[ɝ]　　　　[ɚ]

1.

2.

3.

4.

5.

Travel Experiences
旅遊經驗

I. Topic Preview

1 *Where did you go?* 你去了哪裡？

We went to Italy for a month.

Where did you go in Italy?

We went all over. We visited Rome, Florence, Milan, and Turin.

2 *What did you do?* 你做了什麼事？

Tell me about Rome. What did you do there?

We ate some great local food, and we visited the Colosseum.

3 *Who did you meet?* 你遇到什麼人？

Did you meet any interesting people?

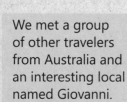

We met a group of other travelers from Australia and an interesting local named Giovanni.

4 *Where did you stay?* 你住在什麼地方？

Did you stay in hostels the whole time? What were the hostels like?

Most of the time, but in Turin we stayed in a little guesthouse. They were fairly basic, but they were really fun places to stay.

5 *What were your impressions?* 你對當地有什麼印象？

What did you think of Italy?

The people were so passionate and friendly.

And the food?

The food was full of local flavor.

And the cities themselves?

Really spectacular. The architecture there was so striking.

II. Vocabulary & Phrases

Spain 西班牙

South Korea 南韓

Brazil 巴西

Japan 日本

France 法國

go to a local festival
參加當地的嘉年華

visit/see a famous sight
參觀／欣賞知名景點

explore the city
探索城市

volunteer on a farm
體驗農場

go on a guided tour
參加旅行團

hotel 飯店

hostel 青年旅社

guesthouse 民宿

campsite 營地

**sleeper car /
couchette** 臥舖車

Sentence Patterns

- Where did you go?
  We went to _France_ for _three weeks_.
- Where in _France_?
  We went all over. / We went to _the south of France_.
- What did you do there?
  We _explored the city_ and _went to a local festival_.
- Did you meet any interesting people?
  Yes, we met _a cool guy named Rodrigo_.
- Where did you stay?
  We stayed in _five-star hotels_. / We slept in _a sleeper car_.
- What was the _guesthouse_ like?
  It was _basic_, but _clean and homey_.
- What did you think of _Spain_?
  The people were so _fun loving_! The food was so _fresh_.
  The scenery/architecture was just _breathtaking_.

123

III. Now, Time to Listen!

1 Nicholas is on vacation in Paris. Listen to him talk on the phone with his mother. Check ☑ the correct boxes to complete the sentences below.

171

PARIS LANDMARKS
巴黎地標

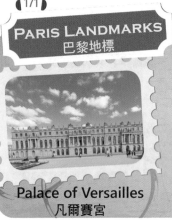
Palace of Versailles
凡爾賽宮

Arc de Triomphe
凱旋門

Eiffel Tower
艾菲爾鐵塔

Champs-Élysées
香榭大道

Moulin Rouge
紅磨坊

A

1 On Monday Nicholas saw . . .

a ☐

b ☐

c ☐

2 Nicholas thought the Palace of Versailles was . . .

a ☐   b ☐   c ☐

B

3 Yesterday, Nicholas went to a . . .

a ☐

b ☐

c ☐

on the Champs-Élysées.

4 Nicholas tried some French . . .

a ☐

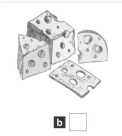
b ☐

c ☐

2 You will hear five people talk about their travel experiences. Match each speaker with the picture that best illustrates his or her experience.

1 _____ 2 _____ 3 _____ 4 _____ 5 _____

(cc by Graham McLellan)

(173) Now, listen again to each speaker and fill in the blanks.

1 The speaker visited _____ for a _____ and went to a _____ called La Tomatina.

2 The speaker _____ on a _____, helped make wine, and lived with the _____.

3 The speaker saw one of the most _____ in the world and _____ many _____.

4 The speaker went traveling in _____ and met all kinds of _____ who _____ weird _____.

5 The speaker explored the city on _____, went _____, and _____ in local _____.

3 Read the descriptions below and listen to Jane talk about her trip to Japan. Then (circle) the correct answers in her online travel updates.

[174]

PLACES TO VISIT WHILE IN TOKYO 東京旅遊景點

karaoke bar 卡拉 OK 歌廳

Imperial Palace 皇居

Harajuku district 原宿區

Tokyo Tower 東京鐵塔

(cc by Hakaishi)

statue of Hachikō 忠犬八公碑

Mount Fuji 富士山

---

1 Just arrived in Japan! Two **ⓐ** months **ⓑ** weeks of fun, here I come!

---

2 Day 1: Went on a **ⓐ** guided tour of Tokyo. **ⓑ** day trip to Mount Fuji.

Saw the **ⓐ** Tokyo Tower **ⓑ** statue of Hachikō and the **ⓐ** Harajuku district. **ⓑ** Imperial Palace.

---

3 Just tried some **ⓐ** sashimi! **ⓑ** sushi! It was so **ⓐ** fresh and delicious! **ⓑ** slimy and disgusting!

---

4 At a **ⓐ** night club **ⓑ** karaoke bar with some local people I met!

---

5 Last day in Tokyo. Catching the **ⓐ** train **ⓑ** bus to Kyoto tonight.

---

6 The **ⓐ** hotels **ⓑ** sleeper cars in Japan are so comfortable! I slept like a baby!

IV. Now, Grammar Time!

Gerunds (V-ing) and
Infinitives (to+V)
動名詞（V-ing）和不定詞（to＋V）
Special Verbs 特殊動詞

remember/forget ⊕	*V-ing* → 記得或忘記一件過去的經驗
	I'll never **forget** *visiting* Spain when I was five.
	to+V → 記得或忘記某件你必須做的事
	I must **remember** *to pack* my camera.
stop ⊕	*V-ing* → 表達被終止的動作
	I **stopped** *following* the tour guide.
	to+V → 表達事情終止的原因
	The plane **stopped** at Bangkok *to refuel*.
try ⊕	*V-ing* → 嘗試是否會成功，或嘗試是否喜歡此事
	I **tried** *volunteering*, but I didn't like it.
	to+V → 嘗試做某件困難或有挑戰性的事
	I **tried** *to climb* Mount Fuji, but it was too high.

❹ Fill in the blanks using the gerund or infinitive form of the verb given under each blank. Remember to read the whole sentence to help you decide which meaning is most suitable.

1 On our guided tour of Tokyo, I stopped many times _____ photos of people
(take)

dressed in crazy clothes.

2 At a local festival in France, I tried _____ a snail, but I just couldn't put it in my
(eat)

mouth!

3 I'll never forget _____ with all those people at the Rio Carnival last year!
(party)

It was so much fun.

4 In Korea, I stopped _____ the spicy food because it hurt my tongue all the time!
(eat)

5 Luckily I remembered _____ a sleeper car on the train. I hate sleeping on those
(book)

uncomfortable train seats.

5 Listen to the following statements, and check ☑ the correct box.

(175)

1 **The speaker** visited Paris last year. ⓐ ☐

is going to visit Paris next year. ⓑ ☐

2 **The speaker** couldn't find a karaoke bar in Tokyo. ⓐ ☐

sang karaoke, but didn't like it. ⓑ ☐

3 **The speaker** explored the city. ⓐ ☐

failed to explore the city. ⓑ ☐

4 **The speaker** stopped because he was lost. ⓐ ☐

started to ask for directions, but didn't finish. ⓑ ☐

5 **The speaker** wrote the postcard yesterday. ⓐ ☐

is going to write a postcard soon. ⓑ ☐

V. Now, Time to Speak!

6 Pair Work! Choose one of the famous places from the next page and discuss it with your partner. Do some research if you need more information.

🔍 Famous Place: _____

| ◀ ▶ | A A | ✂ | + | | · Q▾ |

- famous/beautiful sights and places

  _____

- food

  _____

- activities

  _____

- festivals / parties / markets

  _____

- people you might meet

  _____

- people / scenery / architecture / atmosphere

  _____

Famous Cities 知名城市

Tokyo, Japan 日本東京

Paris, France 法國巴黎

Barcelona, Spain
西班牙巴塞隆納

Krabi, Thailand 泰國喀比

Cairo, Egypt 埃及開羅

Rio de Janeiro, Brazil
巴西里約熱內盧

Activities, Popular Places, and Events 活動、熱門景點與事件

go mountain climbing
爬山

go paragliding
飛行傘

go camel-trekking
騎駱駝

go kayaking
划橡皮艇

see a bullfight 觀賞鬥牛

bazaar 市集商店

full moon party 滿月派對

religious festival 宗教慶典

carnival 嘉年華

night market 夜市

7 Now, with a partner, decide how to fill in the blanks in the following dialogue. Then practice the dialogue with your partner. Share your conversation with the class.

A	_____
B	Wow! That sounds great. Tell me about it.
A	I saw/visited _____.
B	That sounds amazing. What else did you do?
A	I _____, like _____ and _____. They were so tasty.
B	Did you do any fun activities?
A	Oh, yeah. One day I _____!
B	That sounds so exciting! Did you go to any festivals or parties?
A	Yeah, I went to a _____. It was _____. I _____ there. Oh! And I met _____ there, too.
B	Ha! He/She/They sound(s) like a lot of fun. So, what did you think of _____ overall?
A	I thought the _____ was/were _____, the _____ was/were _____, and the _____ was/were really _____.

→ Now, repeat the activity with another place.

8 Have you or your partner ever stayed in one of the places below? If so, tell your partner about the experience. Does anyone in the class have a similar story?

Example   *I stayed in a hotel when I went to Korea last year. It was a five-star hotel. It was luxurious and very expensive. The rooms were huge, and there was a Jacuzzi in the bathroom.*

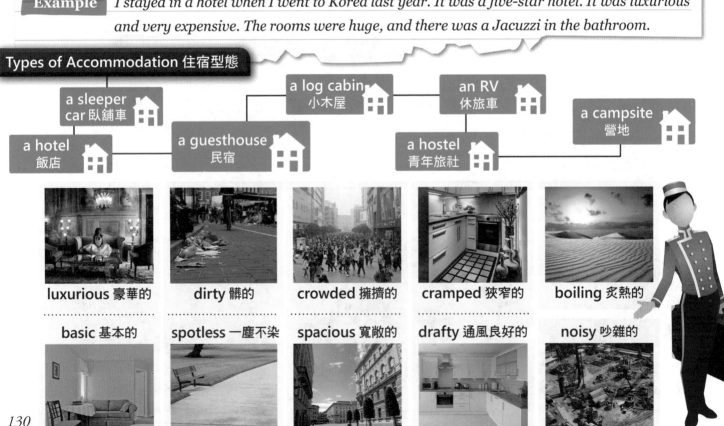

Types of Accommodation 住宿型態

a sleeper car 臥舖車
a log cabin 小木屋
an RV 休旅車
a campsite 營地
a hotel 飯店
a guesthouse 民宿
a hostel 青年旅社

luxurious 豪華的   dirty 髒的   crowded 擁擠的   cramped 狹窄的   boiling 炙熱的

basic 基本的   spotless 一塵不染   spacious 寬敞的   drafty 通風良好的   noisy 吵雜的

9 Listen and repeat the words that you hear.

176

[aɪ]   aisle   high   wise   try   mice

[ɔɪ]   oil   toy   moist   spoil   employ

177   ➡ Listen and ⟨circle⟩ the words that you hear.

1 toil | tile   **2** loiter | lighter   **3** boil | bile   **4** soy | sigh   **5** hoist | heist

10 Listen and repeat the words that you hear.

178

[aʊ]   now   flower   how   mouth   hour

179   ➡ Listen and ⟨circle⟩ the words that you hear.

1 bow | buoy   **2** mouse | mice   **3** trounce | trice   **4** plow | ploy   **5** down | bite

11 Listen to the following sentences. Then read them aloud and write the <u>underlined</u> words in the correct box.

180

→ The <u>tower</u> looked <u>bright</u> against the <u>dour</u> <u>sky</u>.

→ The <u>boys</u> <u>smiled</u> as they ate <u>our</u> <u>boiled</u> <u>koi</u>.

[aɪ]	[ɔɪ]	[aʊ]

At the Airport
機場

I. Topic Preview 181

1 Checking in 辦理報到手續

Is this the check-in desk for flight KL 878?
Do you need to see my e-ticket?

Yes. May I see your passport, please?
Yes, I need to see your booking number.

How many bags will you be checking in?

Just this suitcase, but I also have one carry-on bag.

Could you put your suitcase on the scale, please?

2 Requesting a seat and getting your boarding pass 劃位並領取登機證

Would it be possible to get a window seat?

Let me just check. Yes, there are window seats available. Here's your boarding pass and baggage claim tag.

Thank you. What time does the flight board?

Your flight boards at 9:30 p.m. from Gate D6.

3 Boarding the plane 登機

Passengers with seat numbers 68 to 51 may now start boarding the plane.

This is the final call for passenger David Chang traveling on flight AA 1476. Please proceed immediately to Gate G7 for boarding.

Flight KL 678 to Bangkok will be delayed due to poor weather conditions. More information will be given shortly.

4 Getting through immigration 通過海關

What's the purpose of your visit?

How long do you plan to stay?

Where are you staying?

Do you have a return ticket?

Tourism.

Two weeks.

The Holiday Inn in Oxford.

Yes. Here it is.

II. Vocabulary & Phrases (182)

carry-on bag 手提行李

check-in desk 報到櫃檯

passport 護照

boarding pass 登機證

luggage / baggage / suitcase 行李

baggage claim tag
行李提領證

window seat
靠窗座位

aisle seat
靠走道座位

boarding/departure gate
登機門

conveyor belt
輸送帶

X-ray machine
X 光機

metal detector
金屬探測器

**see-through bag /
transparent bag**
透明袋

liquid items
液體物品

sharp items
尖銳物品

Sentence Patterns (183)

- Is this the check-in desk for flight *KL 878*?
- Do you need to see my *ticket*?
- I'd like to check in this *suitcase*, please.
- I also have one carry-on bag.
  Is this bag OK as a carry-on?
- Would it be possible to get a *window seat*?
- What time does the flight board?
  Your flight boards at *7:45 p.m.*
- At what gate do I board the flight?
  You board the flight at *Gate F5*.

- What's the purpose of your visit?
  Tourism. / I'm here on *business*. / I'm here to *visit family*.
- How long do you plan to stay?
  Three weeks.
- Where are you staying?
  At the *Royal Hotel* in *Birmingham*.
- Do you have a return ticket?
  Yes. Here it is.

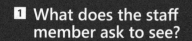 **Now, Time to Listen!**

1 Listen to Paul check in at the airport.
Then answer the questions by checking ☑ the correct box.

1 What does the staff member ask to see?	**2** What kind of seat does Paul request?	**3** How much luggage does Paul have?

a ☐

a ☐

a ☐

b ☐

b ☐

b ☐

 First, take a look at Paul's boarding pass. Now, listen again and fill in the blanks.

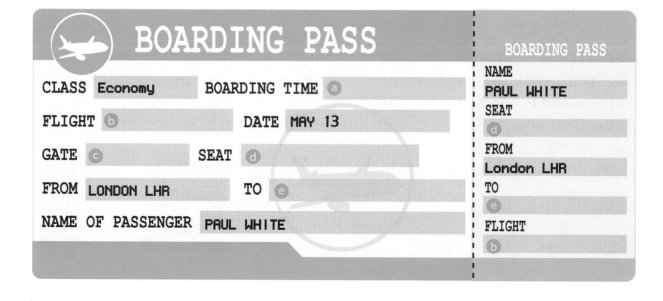

BOARDING PASS

CLASS Economy   BOARDING TIME ⓐ

FLIGHT ⓑ   DATE MAY 13

GATE ⓒ   SEAT ⓓ

FROM LONDON LHR   TO ⓔ

NAME OF PASSENGER PAUL WHITE

BOARDING PASS

NAME
PAUL WHITE
SEAT
ⓓ
FROM
London LHR
TO
ⓔ
FLIGHT
ⓑ

Common Travel Terms
常見旅遊用語

passenger 乘客

business class 商務艙

economy class 經濟艙

passengers requiring assistance
需要協助的乘客

delayed 誤點

canceled 取消

takeoff 起飛

❷ Listen to the announcements and check ☑ the information that's mentioned or implied in each announcement. You may check more than one box for each announcement.

186

1 **ⓐ** ☐ Flight SQ 1476 is flying to London.

ⓑ ☐ The passenger is seated in business class.

ⓒ ☐ The passenger is delaying takeoff.

ⓓ ☐ This announcement will not be repeated.

2 **ⓐ** ☐ The flight is boarding at Gate C9.

ⓑ ☐ The flight time will be 10 hours.

ⓒ ☐ Some passengers can begin boarding the plane.

ⓓ ☐ Passengers will need to show their passports.

3 **ⓐ** ☐ The flight has been canceled.

ⓑ ☐ There is a problem with the aircraft.

ⓒ ☐ The boarding time and gate number have changed.

ⓓ ☐ Passengers will hear more information soon.

187 Listen again and fill in the blanks.

1 Attention, please. This is the _____ call for _____ Henry Lee traveling on Singapore Airlines flight _____ to London. Please proceed immediately to Gate F5 for _____. The plane is ready for _____. Again, this is the final call for passenger Henry Lee.

SINGAPORE AIRLINES

2 Attention, please. American Airlines flight AA 249 to Chicago is now ready for boarding. Passengers traveling with _____ and any passengers _____ special _____ may proceed to board the plane. Please have your boarding _____ and _____ ready for inspection.

AA
AmericanAirlines

3 Attention all passengers on China Airlines flight number CI 547 to Beijing. The _____ has been _____ due to a small technical problem with the aircraft. Boarding _____ for this flight is now 15:35. The _____ gate has also been changed to _____. We apologize for the inconvenience.

CHINA AIRLINES

	too...to	太......以致於不能
	so...that	太......所以

Simple Sentence 簡單句	Complex Sentence 複合句	Meaning 意義
Your suitcase is too *heavy* to take on the plane.	Your suitcase is so *heavy* that you can't take it on the plane.	你不能攜帶你的行李箱上飛機,因為它太重了。
You're too *late* to board the plane.	You're so *late* that you can't board the plane.	你無法登機,因為你遲到了。
This bag is too *big* to fit in the overhead compartment.	This bag is so *big* that it can't fit in the overhead compartment.	這個包包塞不進頭頂置物艙,因為它太大了。

Note Sentences using "so . . . that" emphasize the adjective more than "too . . . to" sentences.
句子使用「so...that」,比使用「too...to」更強調中間的形容詞。

	The bag is so heavy that you can't take it on the plane.	這個行李箱一定超重很多。
	The bag is too heavy to take on the plane.	這個包包可能超重很多,也可能只超重一點點。

3 Pair Work! Alternate reading and changing the simple sentences into complex sentences.

1 The water bottle is too big to fit in the transparent bag.

_____

2 This passport is too old to use.

_____

3 This knife is too dangerous to take on the plane.

_____

4 First-class tickets are too expensive for me to afford.

_____

4 Complete the dialogues using simple sentences and the words given after each blank.

1 A | Would it be possible to get a window seat?

B | I'm sorry, sir. You've checked in _____. *(late)*

2 A | Can I take these scissors in my carry-on bag?

B | I'm sorry. Scissors are _____. *(sharp)*

3 A | Why can't the plane take off?

B | Because of the weather. It's _____. *(windy)*

4 A | Is this the check-in desk for flight AA 342?

136 B | It is, but you're _____. Check-in starts in 30 minutes. *(early)*

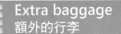 Now, Time to Speak!

Extra baggage
額外的行李

backpack
背包

handbag
手提包

laptop bag
筆電包

camera bag
相機包

excess baggage
超重行李

5 Listen to the following conversation and practice it with your partner. Then look at the departure board and create similar conversations.

188

Traveler	Hello. Is this the check-in desk for flight SQ 578 to Toronto?
Check-in Staff	Yes, sir. May I see your passport, please?
Traveler	Of course. Do you need to see my e-ticket?
Check-in Staff	No, that won't be necessary. Just your passport is fine.
Traveler	Here you are.
Check-in Staff	OK. Thank you. Would you like a window seat or an aisle seat?
Traveler	Could I have a window seat, please?
Check-in Staff	Of course. Seat 23A. And do you have any luggage to check in?
Traveler	Yes, one suitcase. I have a laptop bag, too; is it okay as a carry-on?
Check-in Staff	Yes, that should be fine. Could you put your suitcase on the scale, please?
Traveler	OK.
Check-in Staff	I'm sorry, but the suitcase is two kilograms overweight. You'll need to pay an excess baggage fee of $50.
Traveler	Oh dear. OK. I'll pay with my credit card.
Check-in Staff	All done, sir. Here's your boarding pass and baggage claim tag. Your flight boards at 22:30, and the boarding gate is Gate D8.
Traveler	Thank you very much.

Note: Boarding time is usually around 30-40 minutes before departure time.
注意：登機時間通常是起飛時間的30-40分鐘前。

🛫 Departures			
Time	Flight	Destination	Gate
12:00	OD 1961	BEIJING	06
12:15	PN 0034	TOKYO	18
12:20	T3 0529	DUBAI	32
12:30	PN 2415	HONG KONG	14
12:50	GI 1872	SINGAPORE	09
12:55	T3 0944	BANGKOK	27
13:20	SF 2778	SHANGHAI	20
13:45	OD 0061	SEOUL	31
13:50	BK 1532	KUALA LUMPUR	04
14:05	OD 3487	TAIPEI	12
14:30	PN 0194	OSAKA	03
14:35	SF 0028	JAKARTA	08

6 With a partner, make a list of questions you think an immigration officer would ask a visitor. Compare your list with the class and add any questions you didn't think of.

── Immigration Questions ──

- What's the purpose of your visit?
- How long do you plan to stay?
- Where are you staying?
- Do you have a return ticket?

visa 簽證

tourism / on vacation
旅遊／度假

business / on business
洽公

work / to work 工作

➥ Now, role-play an interview between an immigration officer and a traveler. Would you let the traveler into the country?

visiting relatives /
to visit my family
探望親戚／拜訪家人

138

Now, Time to Pronounce!

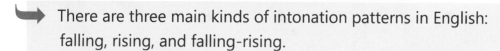

➡ There are three main kinds of intonation patterns in English: falling, rising, and falling-rising.

7 Falling Intonation We use a falling intonation for statements, WH-Questions, (189) and some Question Tags. Listen and repeat the following sentences.

- **Statements** Your bag is too heavy.
- **WH-Questions** What time does your flight leave?
- **Question Tags** The flight's canceled, isn't it?

8 Rising Intonation We use a rising intonation in Yes/No Questions and (190) some Question Tags. Listen and repeat the following sentences.

- **Yes/No Questions** Would you like a window seat?
- **Question Tags** This is OK as a carry-on, isn't it?

9 Falling-Rising We use a falling-rising intonation in statements that are (191) incomplete and to make questions sound more friendly or polite. Listen and repeat the following sentences.

- **Incomplete Statement** I'm here on business, but also to visit family.
- **Polite Questions** Could I get a glass of water, please?

10 Listen, and then practice the following dialogue with a partner. Pay attention to (192) the intonation patterns.

A	Excuse me. Is this the check-in desk for flight KL nine four five?
B	Yes, it is. May I see your passport please?
A	Do you need to see my e-ticket, too?
B	No, that won't be necessary. OK. What kind of seat would you like?
A	I'd like a window seat.
B	No problem.
A	Oh, let me just confirm with you. This bag is OK as a carry-on, isn't it?
B	Yes, it's fine. OK, your flight boards at seven thirty, and your boarding gate is E6.
A	Thank you.

英語力 2

16堂流利英語聽說訓練課
Listening and Speaking in Everyday Life

作　　者	Owain Mckimm
翻　　譯	丁宥榆
英文審訂	Treva Adams
企劃編輯	葉俞均
校　　對	歐寶妮
編　　輯	王鈺婷
內文排版	蔡怡柔／丁宥榆
封面設計	林書玉
製程管理	洪巧玲
發 行 人	黃朝萍
出 版 者	寂天文化事業股份有限公司
電　　話	+886-(0)2-2365-9739
傳　　真	+886-(0)2-2365-9835
網　　址	www.icosmos.com.tw
讀者服務	onlineservice@icosmos.com.tw
出版日期	2024 年 5 月 初版一刷（寂天雲隨身聽 APP 版）

英語力 2：16 堂流利英語聽說訓練課（寂天雲隨身聽
APP 版）/ Owain Mckimm 作；

丁宥榆譯 . -- 初版 . -- [臺北市]：寂天文化，
2024.04- 冊； 公分

ISBN 978-626-300-218-0（菊 8K 平裝）

1.CST: 英語 2.CST: 讀本

805.18　　　　　　　　　　　　112016291

Answer Key, Scripts, and Translation

Unit 01

I Topic Preview p. 8   001

1
This is me when I was a baby.
You were so cute.
Look! I had blond hair back then.

▸ 這是我還是嬰兒的時候。
好可愛喔。
你看，我那時候是金髮。

2
I went to Disneyland when I was seven.
When I was seven, I learned how to swim.

▸ 我七歲的時候去過迪士尼樂園。
我七歲的時候學會游泳。

3
This is Henry VIII.
Who was he?
He was King of England.
When was he king?
He was king from 1509 to 1547.

▸ 這位是亨利八世。
他是誰？
他曾是英國國王。
他在位的時間是何時？
他在位的時間是 1509 到 1547 年。

4
Where did you go on your vacation?
I went to Malaysia.
Did you do anything fun?
I rode an elephant!

▸ 你去哪裡度假？
我去馬來西亞。
你做了什麼好玩的事嗎？
我騎了大象！

5
What did you do on Saturday night?
I just stayed home and watched a movie.
- -
On Sunday I played soccer with my friends.
I made dinner for my boyfriend.

▸ 你星期六晚上在做什麼？
我只有在家看電影。
- -
星期天我和朋友去踢足球。
我為我男朋友做晚餐。

Sentence Patterns   003 p. 9

- 我昨天／昨天晚上／上個禮拜在家裡看電視。
- 去年暑假／兩個禮拜前／五年前／十年前我去馬來西亞。
- 他生於一百多年前／兩千年前。
- 我四歲／七歲／十歲的時候學會游泳。
- 我畢業於 2007／1975 年。

III Now, Time to Listen! p. 10

1
1 Michael Jackson   004
2 Confucius
3 William Shakespeare

Script & Translation

1

Peter	OK, I'm ready. You can start asking questions.
Janet	Um. Was he a philosopher?
Peter	No, he wasn't.
Janet	Was he a musician?
Peter	Yes, he was. He was a great dancer, too.
Janet	Hmm. Did he live in America?
Peter	Yes, he did.
Janet	I think I know! Person A is . . .

彼德	好，我準備好了。你可以開始發問。
珍妮特	嗯，他是哲學家嗎？
彼德	不是。
珍妮特	他是音樂家嗎？
彼德	對，他是。他也是一名厲害的舞者。
珍妮特	唔，他住在美國嗎？
彼德	沒錯。
珍妮特	那我知道了！人物 A 就是……

2

Janet	OK, my turn. Start guessing.
Peter	Did he live in England?
Janet	No.
Peter	France?
Janet	No.
Peter	OK, tell me. Where did he live?
Janet	He lived in China.
Peter	And when did he die?
Janet	He died over 2,000 years ago.
Peter	OK. Was he a famous philosopher?
Janet	Yes, he was.
Peter	I know. Person B is . . .

| 珍妮特 | 好，換我了。開始猜吧。 |
| 彼德 | 他住在英國嗎？ |

1

珍妮特	不是。	
彼德	法國？	
珍妮特	不是。	
彼德	好吧，告訴我吧，他到底住在哪裡？	
珍妮特	他住在中國。	
彼德	他死於什麼時候？	
珍妮特	他死於兩千多年前。	
彼德	好，那麼他是知名的哲學家嗎？	
珍妮特	是的。	
彼德	我知道了，人物 B 就是……	

3

Peter	My turn again.
Janet	OK, let me think. Did he make movies?
Peter	No, but he wrote a lot of famous plays.
Janet	Ah, this one's easy. Was he from England?
Peter	Yes!
Janet	Did he write *Romeo and Juliet*?
Peter	Yes! I think you've got it.
Janet	Person C is . . .

彼德	又換我了。
珍妮特	好，讓我想一想。他是拍電影的嗎？
彼德	不是，但是他寫過很多知名的劇本。
珍妮特	啊，這個簡單。他是不是英國人？
彼德	沒錯！
珍妮特	他是不是寫過《羅蜜歐與茱莉葉》？
彼德	對！我想你知道是誰了。
珍妮特	人物 C 就是……

2 🅐 **1** a   **2** b   🎧005
🅑 **3** b   **4** c   **5** a   🎧006

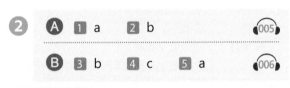

Script & Translation

🅐
Angela	Hello Paul. Did you have a good weekend?
Paul	Yes, it was great. I went shopping and bought lots of new clothes.
Angela	Oh. Did you spend a lot of money?
Paul	Well, I spent $200. Is that a lot?
Angela	Wow! That was a good shopping trip!

安潔拉	哈囉，保羅。你上個週末過得好不好？
保羅	很好，我去逛街，還買了好多新衣服。
安潔拉	喔，你花了很多錢嗎？
保羅	嗯，我花了 200 美金，那樣算多嗎？
安潔拉	哇！你買得很過癮耶！

🅑
Paul	So what did you do? Anything interesting?
Angela	Yes, actually. I went to a party on Saturday night.
Paul	That sounds like fun! Did you meet anyone?
Angela	Yeah, I did. I met an actor called Dan. He was really cool.
Paul	What did you guys talk about?
Angela	We talked about movies we like . . . oh, and basketball.
Paul	Basketball?
Angela	Yeah. When Dan was in school, he was a basketball player.

保羅	那你做了些什麼？有什麼好玩的嗎？
安潔拉	有喔。我星期六晚上去了一個派對。
保羅	好像很好玩！你有遇到誰嗎？
安潔拉	有，我遇到一個叫作丹的演員，他好酷。
保羅	你們聊了些什麼？
安潔拉	我們聊一些我們喜愛的電影……喔，還有籃球。
保羅	籃球？
安潔拉	對啊，丹以前在學校是籃球選手。

3 **2** Laura – a – 3   🎧007
   3 Maurice – e – 4
   4 Sarah – c – 5
   5 Robert – b – 2

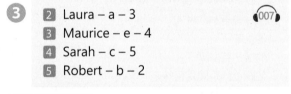

Script & Translation

1 Hi, I'm James. When I was five, my dad gave me a new bike. It was bright red. I rode it every day.
嗨，我是詹姆斯。我五歲的時候，爸爸給我一台新的腳踏車，是亮紅色的，我每天都會騎它。

2 Hi, I'm Laura. My mom taught me how to swim when I was seven. That was in 1996.
嗨，我是蘿拉。七歲的時候，我媽媽教我游泳，那是 1996 年的事了。

3 I'm Maurice. When I was 10 years old, I went on vacation to Hawaii with my family. We sunbathed all day on the beach.
我是墨利斯。我十歲的時候，和家人去夏威夷度假，我們一整天都在海灘上做日光浴。

4 My name's Sarah. When I was 15 years old, my family and I went to the seaside. We swam in the sea all day.
我的名字叫莎拉。我 15 歲的時候，和家人一起去海邊，我們一整天都在海裡游泳。

5 Hi, I'm Robert. In 1987 I fell off my bike and cut my leg. It hurt so much that I cried for hours.

嗨，我是羅伯特。1987 年時，我騎腳踏車摔車，割傷了腿，痛得我哭了好幾個小時。

IV Now, Grammar Time! p. 12

4
Regular Verbs
1 jumped 2 cleaned 3 hiked
4 sunbathed 5 visited 6 rested

Irregular Verbs
1 bought 2 went 3 drank
4 saw 5 met 6 swam

5
2 Lena and Drew went hiking
3 Drew went diving in the ocean
4 Lena went shopping
5 Lena and Drew rested on the beach

V Now, Time to Speak! p. 14

7
 Translation 008

A 好，我準備好了。
B 第一個問題：他是男生嗎？
A 對，他是。
B 他是運動員嗎？
A 不是。
B 好，那他是做什麼的？
A 他是藝術家，但他也發明了很多東西。
B 唔，他是義大利人嗎？
A 是的。
B 〈蒙娜麗莎的微笑〉是他畫的嗎？
A 沒錯。
B 他是李奧納多・達文西嗎？
A 答對了！

8
 Translation 009

麥克　你昨天晚上去哪裡了？
蒂娜　我去參加朋友的慶生會，為什麼這樣問？
麥克　我打電話去你家，你不在。慶生會好玩嗎？
蒂娜　很好玩。你昨天晚上有做什麼有趣的事嗎？
麥克　沒有耶，就煮晚餐，然後看書。

VI Now, Time to Pronounce! p. 15

9
[d]　1, 3, 4　011
[t]　1, 5, 6　012

11
2 [d]　3 [ɪd]　4 [t]　014
5 [d]　6 [ɪd]　7 [d]
8 [d]　9 [ɪd]　10 [t]

Unit 02

I Topic Preview p. 16　015

1 I love this fish. How's your beef?
It's perfect.

▸ 我很喜歡這道魚，你的牛肉怎麼樣？
非常好吃。

2 I'm not too keen on this salad.
I don't like these vegetables at all.

▸ 我不是很愛這沙拉。
我一點也不愛這些蔬菜。

3 What do you think of this coat?
I like the style, but I don't like the color.

▸ 你覺得這件外套怎麼樣？
我覺得樣式不錯，但是我不喜歡這個顏色。

4 Math class is the worst! I really hate it.
I don't like math either, but I love history.
Science is my favorite class.

▸ 數學課最討厭了！我真恨數學。
我也不喜歡數學，可是我愛歷史。
科學是我最喜歡的一門課。

5 Do you like horror movies?
No. Horror movies are the worst!

Action movies are my favorite.
I'm not a big fan of action movies.

▸ 你喜歡看恐怖片嗎？
不喜歡，恐怖片最難看了！

我最喜歡看動作片了。
我不怎麼愛看動作片。

Sentence Patterns

- 我愛吃海鮮。　我愛藝術課。　我痛恨愛情片。
- 我不喜歡吃蔬菜。　我不是很愛數學課。
  我不愛看喜劇片。　我受不了體育課。
- 英文（課）太有趣了！　科幻片最難看。
  海鮮還可以。
- 我最喜愛的電影類型是動作片。
  我最喜歡的課程是科學和數學。
  牛肉是我最愛吃的食物。
  科幻片是我最喜愛的電影類型。
  數學和英文是我最喜歡的課程。
- （跟動作片比起來）我比較愛看恐怖片。

III Now, Time to Listen!
p. 18

1　1 F　2 T　3 F　4 T　5 T　018

Script & Translation

Mark	Hi Jane. Do you want to go see a movie tonight?
Jane	Sure. I love horror movies. Let's go see one of those.
Mark	Horror movies? No, thanks. I hate getting scared. I prefer comedies.
Jane	You're such a baby! But comedies are OK, I guess. All right, let's go see a comedy.

馬克	嗨，珍，你今天晚上想不想去看電影？
珍	好啊，我愛恐怖片，我們去看恐怖片。
馬克	恐怖片？不用了，謝謝，我最痛恨被嚇了。我比較想看喜劇片。
珍	你很孩子氣耶！不過喜劇片也可以啦。好吧，我們去看喜劇片。

2　1 ⓐ likes　　ⓑ dislikes　019
　　　 ⓒ likes　　 ⓓ favorite
　　 2 ⓐ favorite　ⓑ dislikes
　　　 ⓒ worst　　 ⓓ likes

Script & Translation

1 Hi, I'm Peter. I go to St. John's High School. I'm a pretty good student, and I like studying. I like science, but I don't like gym class because I hate running. I like English, too, but I prefer math. Math class is my favorite actually.

嗨，我是彼德。我就讀於聖約翰高中，我是個很好的學生，很愛讀書。我喜歡科學，不愛體育課，因為我痛恨跑步。我也喜歡英文，但我更愛數學，老實說，數學課是我的最愛。

2 The school lunches here are great. I just love it when we get Italian food. Pasta is my favorite. I'm not too keen on the vegetables they serve here, though. Oh, and the seafood is the worst! But we do get donuts for dessert, and I like donuts a lot.

這裡的學校午餐很棒，我最愛義大利菜，我最喜歡義大利麵。可是我不怎麼愛吃這裡供應的蔬菜。噢，海鮮最難吃了！不過點心會有甜甜圈，我很愛吃甜甜圈。

3　1 c　2 e　3 b　4 d　5 a　020

Script & Translation

1 Hi, I'm Dan. I really love funny movies, but I can't stand romantic movies. They make me want to puke!

嗨，我是丹。我真的很愛看搞笑片，我很受不了愛情片。愛情片讓我很想吐！

2 Hi, I'm Wanda. My favorite thing about school is gym class. I just love to exercise. I can't do math, though. I hate it. It's just too hard.

嗨，我是汪妲。學校裡我最喜歡體育課，我很愛運動。不過我不會算數學，我恨數學，它太難了。

3 Hi, I'm John. I like to wear the color black. I think it makes me look cool. I hate wearing bright colors.

嗨，我是約翰。我喜歡穿黑色衣服，我覺得那讓我看起來很酷。我討厭穿鮮豔的顏色。

4 Hi, I'm Jenny. I love to dress up in bright colors. Red skirts, purple hats—the brighter the better! I just can't stand people who wear only black.

嗨，我是珍妮，我喜歡穿顏色鮮豔的衣服，紅裙啦、紫色帽子啦——越鮮豔越好！我實在受不了那些只穿黑色衣服的人。

5 Hi, I'm Kate. I think action movies are really boring. I like comedies, though, and horror movies, too. I love movies that make me jump.

嗨，我是凱特。我覺得動作片好無聊，不過我喜歡喜劇片和恐怖片，能讓我跳起來的片子我都愛。

IV Now, Grammar Time!
p. 19

4　ⓑ enjoys swimming
　　 ⓒ doesn't like vegetables
　　 ⓓ enjoys music
　　 ⓔ likes animals
　　 ⓕ likes to climb trees

5
1. going 2. dancing
3. reading | reading / to read
4. studying / to study | likes science class
5. watching | watching / to watch

V Now, Time to Speak!
p. 21

6

🎧 Translation (021)

A
男 | 我覺得你戴那頂帽子很好看。
女 | 真的嗎？我不喜歡這個顏色。
男 | 那或許你可以試試這頂紅色的。
女 | 好，我很喜歡那一頂。

B
男 | 你的牛排如何？好吃嗎？
女 | 不好吃，我很不喜歡，牛排沒熟。
男 | 噢，不會吧！我的義大利麵很好吃耶，味
道很棒。
女 | 我可以吃一些你的嗎？我喜歡義大利菜。
男 | 嗯，我覺得這樣不太好。

VI Now, Time to Pronounce!
p. 23

10
1. [z] [s] [s]
2. [s] [s] [z] [z]
3. [z] [s] [z]
4. [s] [s] [z] [z]
(025)

11
[f] 1, 9, 12   [v] 5, 8, 11
[s] 3, 4, 10   [z] 2, 6, 7
(026)

Unit 03

I Topic Preview
p. 24 (027)

1
I'm having a party next week. Do you want to come?
Sure. I'll be there.
It's going to be so much fun.
I'll bring all my friends.

▸ 下星期我要辦一場派對，你要來嗎？
好啊，我會去。
一定會超好玩的。
我會帶我所有的朋友去。

2
What are you planning on doing after graduating?
I'm planning on going traveling for a few months. You?
I'm getting a job at my dad's company.

▸ 你畢業後打算做什麼？
我打算去旅行幾個月，你呢？
我要去我爸的公司上班。

3
I'm going on vacation next week.
How long are you going for?
I'm going for three weeks.
Where are you going?
I'm going to Spain for a week and then to France for two weeks.

▸ 我下個禮拜要去度假。
你要去多久？
我要去三個禮拜。
你要去哪裡呢？
我要去西班牙一個禮拜，然後再去法國兩個禮拜。

4
What are your plans for Christmas?
I'm planning to spend time with my family.

▸ 聖誕節你有什麼計畫？
我打算和我家人在一起過節。

5
Are you getting James something for his birthday?
Yes, I am. I'm going to buy him a gift tomorrow.

▸ 你會送詹姆斯生日禮物嗎？
會，我明天要去買送給他的禮物。

Sentence Patterns
(029) p. 25

• 你這個星期六要做什麼？
我要舉辦派對。
• 你聖誕節打算做什麼？
我聖誕節打算回去看我家人。
• 你今年夏天會去旅遊嗎？
會。／不會。
• 你畢業後打算要工作嗎？
要。／不要。

III Now, Time to Listen!
p. 26

1
1. d 2. b 3. a 4. e 5. c

(030)

🎧 Script & Translation

1 OK, I know this sounds crazy, but after I leave school, I'm planning on opening my own candy store.

好，我知道這聽起來很瘋狂，但是等我畢業之後，我計畫要開自己的糖果店。

2 I really love music, so when I graduate, I'm going to play guitar in a band.

我太愛音樂了，所以等我畢業之後，我要加入樂團彈吉他。

3 Well, I want to be a history teacher, so I'm planning on studying history at university.

我想當歷史老師，所以我大學打算修歷史。

4 I'm planning on traveling to Europe. I want to see all the sights!

我計畫要去歐洲旅行，我想要看遍風景名勝！

5 I'm going to write a book and become a famous author.

我要寫書，當知名作家。

2

Tuesday	have dinner with mom and dad	(031)
Friday	hang out with friends	
Saturday	go on vacation to Egypt	

Script & Translation

I'm going to be very busy next month. On Monday the second I'm playing tennis with my brother. On Tuesday the third I'm going to have dinner with my mom and dad. On Friday the sixth I'm going to hang out with my friends. On Saturday the 14th, I'm going on vacation to Egypt.

我下個月會很忙。2 號星期一，我要和我哥打網球。3 號星期二，我要和我父母吃晚飯。6 號星期五，我要和朋友出去。14 號星期六，我要去埃及旅行。

1 – 4 – 5 – 2 – 3 (032)

Script & Translation

I'm planning to see the pyramids on the 16th and then visit some museums on the 17th. On the 18th I'm planning on riding a camel in the desert. On the 19th I'm going on a boat down the River Nile. I'm coming home on the 21st.

我計畫 16 號參觀金字塔，17 號參觀一些博物館，18 號去沙漠騎駱駝，19 號乘船遊尼羅河，21 號回家。

3 | ⓐ Sam | ⓑ Lucy | ⓒ Josh | (033)

1 next week, What are		(034)
2 going to	**3** getting	**4** is planning

Script & Translation

Sam | OK. It's Emma's birthday next week. What are you planning to get her, Lucy?

Lucy | Emma loves music, so I'm going to get her a CD. How about you Sam?

Sam | I don't know. Um, I'm either getting her a book or a watch. But I'm not sure which one's best.

Lucy | Oh no! Josh is planning to buy her a watch. He told me last week that Emma needs a new one.

Sam | OK. No problem. Josh can get her a watch. I'll get her a book.

山姆 | 好，下週就是艾瑪的生日了，露西，你打算買什麼送她？

露西 | 艾瑪熱愛音樂，所以我要送她一片 CD，山姆，你呢？

山姆 | 我不知道，嗯，我會買書或手錶送她吧，可是我不確定送哪一個比較好。

露西 | 噢，不行！喬許要送她手錶，他上個星期才跟我說艾瑪需要一支新手錶。

山姆 | 好吧，沒關係。喬許可以送她手錶，我送書。

IV Now, Grammar Time! p. 27

4
2 Are, going to, am going to
3 Will, will
4 will, am going to, Will, am going to
5 will, am going to

5
3 He's going to buy a cake.
4 He's going to buy lots of food.
5 He's going to invite Emma's friends.
6 He isn't going to invite Emma's parents.
7 He isn't going to hire a DJ.
8 He's going to borrow Sam's CD player.
9 He's going to buy balloons.

V Now, Time to Speak! p. 29

7
Translation (035)

1 A | 我下個禮拜要辦聖誕派對，你要不要來？
B | 好啊，謝謝你邀請我。時間和地點呢？
A | 12 月 24 號在我家。
B | 我需要帶什麼嗎？
A | 帶一些禮物來就可以了，我們午夜的時候要交換禮物。

2 A | 我打算下個週末要去看表演，你要不要一起去？

B	好啊，在哪裡？
A	在阿爾巴尼路的一間夜店，我最愛的一個樂團要表演。
B	好酷，還有誰會去嗎？
A	有，我妹妹也會一起去。

VI Now, Time to Pronounce! p. 31

9 [θ] three, toothbrushes, thought 037
　 [ð] There, brother's, They, the, other

11 1 heat　 2 ill　 3 arm 041
　 4 hair　 5 hedge

Unit 04

I Topic Preview p. 32 042

1　The Bears are a much better team than the Tigers.
　 I totally disagree. The Tigers are the better team.
　 Our players are faster, stronger, and fitter than yours.
　 Yes, but our players have more heart.

▶ 熊隊比虎隊強多了。
　我完全不同意，虎隊比較強。
　我們的球員速度比你們快，也比你們強壯和健康。
　是沒錯，但是我們的球員比較有心。

2　Excuse me. Which computer do you think is better?
　 Well, this one's faster and has more memory, but it's more expensive.

▶ 不好意思，請問你覺得哪一台電腦比較好？
　嗯，這一台的速度比較快，記憶體也比較大，但是比較貴。

3　Are you taller than Mike?
　 He's taller than me.

▶ 你比麥克高嗎？
　他比我高。

4　How is Taiwan different from England?
　 Taiwan is much hotter than England, but the food is more delicious in Taiwan.

▶ 台灣和英國有什麼不同？
　台灣比英國熱，但是台灣的食物比較好吃。

5　I'm the smartest student in my class.
　 Nina says she's the fastest runner on the team.
　 Jack thinks he's the most talented actor in the world.

▶ 我是我們班最聰明的學生。
　妮娜說她是隊上跑得最快的人。
　傑克認為他是全世界最有天賦的演員。

Sentence Patterns 044 p. 33

- （跟他比起來）我比較高。
- （相較於電影）書比較有趣。
- （跟我比起來）湯姆和吉姆的年紀比較大。
- （跟那支比起來）這支智慧型手機的速度比較快。
- （跟另一台比起來）這台電腦的記憶體比較大。
- （跟你比起來）我比較有錢。
- 你覺得哪一支球隊比較好？
- 台灣和日本有何不同？／
  台灣跟日本比起來有何不同？
- 印度比英國熱嗎？
- 你比珍妮聰明嗎？
- 我是全校最帥的男生。
- 她是全世界最優秀的網球選手。

III Now, Time to Listen! p. 34

1　1 black, brown　 2 smarter 045
　 3 bag, heavier　 4 the most beautiful
　 5 more talented

Script & Translation

1 | W | Which shoes are better, the black ones or the brown ones?
　| M | I think the black ones are much better. They're cheaper, too.
　| 女 | 哪一雙鞋比較好看，黑色的還是咖啡色的？
　| 男 | 我覺得黑色的好看得多，而且也比較便宜。

2 | M | Jane, do you want some help with your math homework?
　| W | No, thanks. I can do it myself. I'm smarter than you think, Dad.
　| 男 | 珍，你的數學作業需要人幫忙嗎？
　| 女 | 不用，謝謝，我自己可以寫。我比你想像中的聰明，老爸。

3 | M | Why do I always have to carry the heavier bag?
　| W | Are you kidding? This bag is much heavier than that one.

| 男 | 為什麼每次都是我拿比較重的一袋？ |
| 女 | 你開玩笑嗎？這一袋比那一袋還重耶。 |

4
W	So, who do you think is America's most beautiful actress?
M	I think Angelina Jolie's the most beautiful. You?
女	你覺得美國最美的女演員是誰？
男	我覺得最美的是安潔莉娜・裘莉，你呢？

5
M	So, why do you think you should get the job?
W	I think I'm the best person for the job because I'm the most talented.
男	所以，你為什麼認為自己應該被錄取？
女	我認為我是這份工作的最佳人選，因為我是最有才華的。

2
1. Tom – Simon – Daz
2. Daz – Tom – Simon
3. Simon – Tom – Daz
4. Simon – Daz – Tom

(046)

Script & Translation

1 Simon is taller than Daz, but Tom is taller than Simon.
賽門比達茲高，湯姆又比賽門高。

2 Daz is the heaviest, and Tom is heavier than Simon.
達茲是最重的，而湯姆比賽門重。

3 Simon is older than Tom and Daz. Daz is the youngest.
賽門的年紀比湯姆和達茲大，達茲是最年輕的。

4 Daz is smarter than Tom, but he's not smarter than Simon.
達茲比湯姆聰明，但是他沒有賽門聰明。

3   **1** b **2** a **3** a **4** b   (047)

Script & Translation

1
A	Hello. I'd like to book a vacation, please.
B	Of course, sir. Where would you like to go?
A	I'd like to go to Singapore or Japan, but I'm not sure which one. I'd prefer somewhere cold.
B	Well, at this time of year, Japan is colder than Singapore.
A	OK, great. I'll take a . . .
A	哈囉，我想要預訂一個度假行程。
B	沒問題，先生。請問您想去哪裡？
A	我想去新加坡或日本，但還不確定。我比較想去冷一點的地方。

| B | 每年的這個時候，日本比新加坡冷。 |
| A | 好，太好了。那我要……。 |

2
A	Hello. I'd like to buy a ticket for a movie.
B	OK, no problem. Which movie?
A	Are there any scary movies showing today?
B	Yes, there are two: *Ghost House 2* and *Vampire Blood 3*.
A	Which one's scarier? I love really scary movies.
B	Everyone says that *Ghost House 2* is scarier than *Vampire Blood 3*.
A	Great. I'll take a ticket for . . .
A	哈囉，我要買一張電影票。
B	好的，沒問題，哪一部電影？
A	今天有恐怖片嗎？
B	有兩部：《鬼屋 2》和《血戰吸血鬼 3》。
A	哪一部比較恐怖？我很喜歡很恐怖的那種。
B	大家都說《鬼屋 2》比《血戰吸血鬼 3》恐怖。
A	太好了，我要買一張……的票。

3
A	Excuse me. I want to buy a science book for my son.
B	Sure. These two books are our most popular: *UFOs* and *Ocean Life*.
A	Hmm. Which one do you think is more interesting?
B	Personally, I think *UFOs* is more interesting, but *Ocean Life* is easier to read.
A	Oh, that's OK. My son is pretty smart. I'll take . . .
A	不好意思，我要買一本科學書籍給我兒子。
B	好的，這兩本是我們最暢銷的：《飛碟奧秘》和《海洋世界》。
A	唔，你覺得哪一本比較有趣？
B	我個人認為《飛碟奧秘》比較有趣，但是《海洋世界》比較易讀。
A	喔，沒關係，我兒子很聰明。那我就買……。

4
A	Hello. I'd like to buy a new car. Do you have any really fast ones?
B	We have these two right here. This red car is actually faster than the blue one, but the blue one is smaller, so it's more convenient if you live in the city.
A	I do live in the city. OK, I think I'd better get the smaller one. I'll take the . . .
A	哈囉，我要買一輛新車，你們有沒有速度夠快的？

B 我們這裡有這兩輛，紅色的這一輛其實比藍色的快，但是藍色的比較小，在都市裡駕駛更方便。

A 我的確是住在都市。好吧，我想我還是買小的好了。那我要買……。

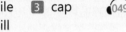 **Now, Grammar Time!**　p. 35

4　② is less famous　③ is more dangerous
　④ is less exciting　⑤ is more comfortable

5　① highest　② fastest　③ richest
　④ tallest　⑤ oldest

Ⅵ Now, Time to Pronounce!　p. 39

9　① breeze　② bile　③ cap　(049)
　④ bear　⑤ bill

11　① [p]　② [t]　③ [b]　④ [t]　(052)
　⑤ [d]　⑥ [p]　⑦ [d]　⑧ [t]

Script
① pencil　② taint　③ bowling　④ till
⑤ rend　⑥ pan　⑦ dingy　⑧ tight

Unit 05

Ⅰ Topic Preview　(053)　p. 40

1 Hi, I think we have a mutual friend.
Oh, really? Who?
Peter Jones. I think he works with you.
Yes! How do you know him?
He's my brother-in-law.

▶ 嗨，我們好像有共同的朋友喔。
喔，真的嗎？誰？
彼德‧瓊斯，他好像是你同事。
對！你怎麼會認識他？
他是我小舅子。

2 Did you hear the news about Simon?
No. What happened?
He left his job and went to live in Antarctica!

▶ 你有聽到關於賽門的事嗎？
沒有，什麼事？
他辭職搬去南極住了！

3 How's Anthony's mother? I heard she's not well.
Yeah, she hurt herself pretty badly.

▶ 安東尼的媽媽怎麼了？我聽說她身體不舒服。
對啊，她傷得滿嚴重的。

4 I need to find a singer for my band.
How about my friend Daniel?
Can he sing?
Yeah, he sings beautifully.

▶ 我的樂團需要找一位主唱。
我的朋友丹尼爾如何？
他會唱嗎？
會，他唱歌很好聽。

Sentence Patterns　(055)　p. 41

- 我們有一位共同的朋友。
- 你是怎麼認識珍的？
- 布萊德利是我的同事，我們一起踢足球。
  嘉絲敏是我的朋友，我們在舞蹈課上認識的。
- 你有聽到關於保羅的消息嗎？
- 發生什麼事了？／快跟我講八卦！
- 看樣子，約翰的叔叔被逮捕了。
  我聽說麗姿發生意外了。
- 我要找一位室友。
  我的同事傑洛米如何？

Ⅲ Now, Time to Listen!　p. 42

1　② colleague　③ babysitter　(056)
　④ distant relative　⑤ friend of the family

Script & Translation

1	Rachael	Hi, Bill. Do you know Sam Crooks? I think he's a mutual friend of ours.
	Bill	Yes, I do know him. He's my roommate.
	瑞秋	嗨，比爾。你認識山姆‧克魯克斯嗎？他好像是我們的共同朋友。
	比爾	認識啊，他是我室友。
2	Mandy	Hello, I'm Mandy.
	Bill	Hi, I'm Bill. I've heard about you actually.
	Mandy	Oh? From whom?
	Bill	From my colleague Peter Smith. You're his cousin, right?

曼蒂	哈囉，我是曼蒂。
比爾	嗨，我是比爾。其實我聽説過你。
曼蒂	哦？誰提過我？
比爾	我的同事彼德·史密斯，你是他表妹，對嗎？

3

Sarah	Bill, do you know Nick Brown?
Bill	Yes, I do actually. He's my daughter's babysitter.
Sarah	Great. Can you give him a message for me?

莎拉	比爾，你認識尼克·布朗嗎？
比爾	我的確認識他，他是我女兒的保母。
莎拉	太好了，你可以幫我傳話給他嗎？

4

Bill	Charlotte, hi!
Charlotte	Hi, Bill. I met one of your friends last night at a party.
Bill	Oh, really? Who?
Charlotte	Robert Wells.
Bill	Oh, Robert! He's actually a distant relative of mine.

比爾	嗨，夏綠蒂！
夏綠蒂	嗨，比爾。我在昨晚的派對遇到你的朋友耶。
比爾	哦，真的嗎？誰啊？
夏綠蒂	羅伯特·威爾斯。
比爾	喔，羅伯特！他其實是我的遠房親戚。

5

Grace	Bill, I think I play tennis with a friend of yours.
Bill	Yes, I know. Jenny, right? Jenny Bond.
Grace	Yeah. She says hi. How do you know her?
Bill	Oh, she's an old friend of the family.

葛瑞絲	比爾，我好像和你的朋友一起打網球耶。
比爾	是啊，我知道。珍妮嘛，對嗎？
葛瑞絲	沒錯，她説要向你問好。你是怎麼認識她的？
比爾	喔，她是我們家的老朋友了。

2 ❷ M ❸ G ❹ R ❺ D (057)
❻ G ❼ D ❽ M

Script & Translation

1 I know. My friend John's the perfect person for you. He can fix anything.
我知道了，我朋友約翰是最佳人選，他什麼都會修。

2 Yes, I know Sam. He's my neighbor.
是啊，我認識山姆，他是我的鄰居。

3 Did you hear about Jenny? She's dating her boss!
你有聽到珍妮的事嗎？她跟她老闆約會耶！

4 My cousin Peter can act really well. You should use him in your show.
我表哥彼德很會演戲喔，你的表演節目可以用他。

5 How's Rob's leg? I heard he broke it.
羅伯的腿還好嗎？我聽説他的腿斷了。

6 Oh my God! Did he really dump her? No wonder I saw him with another girl.
噢，天啊！他真的甩了她？難怪我看到他跟另一個女生在一起。

7 Nick's not doing too well recently. He just lost his job.
尼克最近不太順利，他剛失業。

8 I know Bill from my English class.
我是在英文課認識比爾的。

3 ❶ a ❷ a, c ❸ a, b (058)

Script & Translation

1

| Mark | Do you know Sarah Connor? |
| Diane | Yes. We're on the same basketball team. How do you know her? |

| 馬克 | 你認識莎拉·康納嗎？ |
| 黛安 | 認識，我們是同一支籃球隊的，你怎麼會認識她？ |

2

| Emily | I work with Sarah at the restaurant. She's great. Everyone at the restaurant loves her. She works really hard, and she's always smiling happily. |

| 愛蜜麗 | 我跟莎拉一起在餐廳上班，她很棒，餐廳裡人人都喜歡她。而且她工作很認真，總是面帶燦爛的笑容。 |

3

| Elaine | I'm not surprised, but she talks so loudly sometimes. Don't people get angry with her? |
| Adam | She's loud, but she always behaves politely, so no one gets mad at her. |

| 依蓮 | 我不意外，不過有時候講話真的很大聲，都沒有人生氣嗎？ |
| 亞當 | 她的嗓門是很大，不過她總是彬彬有禮，所以沒有人生她的氣。 |

IV Now, Grammar Time!

p. 43

4
- 2 messily
- 3 easily
- 4 safely
- 5 patiently
- 6 automatically
- 7 well
- 8 loudly

5
- 2 quickly / hurriedly
- 3 loudly / happily
- 4 messily / greedily
- 5 late
- 6 smartly / well / professionally
- 7 beautifully / neatly / tidily
- 8 crazily / angrily
- 9 well / energetically / seriously

V Now, Time to Speak!

p. 45

6

Translation

A A 你認識會修電腦的人嗎？
059 B 認識，我的朋友鮑伯會，他是修電腦快手。
B A 你認識丹·瓊斯嗎？
060 B 認識，他是我隊友，我們練習足球的時候認識的。你呢？
A 他是我同事，我們一起工作。

8

Translation 061

傑洛米 明蒂，你有聽説班的事嗎？
明蒂 沒有，他怎麼了？
傑洛米 聽説他甩了他女朋友。
明蒂 不會吧！他上個星期還跟我説想娶她耶！
傑洛米 不過，他昨天晚上帶了別的女生去詹姆斯的派對。
明蒂 噢，天啊！

VI Now, Time to Pronounce!

p. 47

9

[k] keep, kitchen, cupboard, can, careful, pink 063

[g] girl's, gold, golf, garden, gate 064

10
- 1 [tʃ]
- 2 [dʒ]
- 3 [dʒ]
- 4 [tʃ]
- 5 [tʃ]
- 6 [dʒ]
066

Script

- 1 champ
- 2 gym
- 3 jail
- 4 cheat
- 5 check
- 6 join

Unit 06

I Topic Preview

p. 48 067

1
Excuse me. Where can I find the fresh fruit?
Fresh fruit is on aisle five. I'll show you.
Thank you. Oh, do you have any shampoo in stock?
No, I'm sorry. We're sold out.

▸ 不好意思，請問哪裡可以找到新鮮水果？
新鮮水果在第五走道，我帶您去。
謝謝。喔，你們有賣洗髮精嗎？
沒有，不好意思，賣完了。

2
Can I try this in a bigger size?
Of course. What size do you want to try?
Size 12, please.

▸ 我可以試穿這件大一點的尺寸嗎？
當然可以，您想要試什麼尺寸？
12 號。

3
Do you have this in a different color?
What color do you want to try?
Green, please.

▸ 這個有其他顏色嗎？
您想要試什麼顏色？
綠色。

4
How much is this?
That's $100.
That's way too expensive. I'll give you $50 for it.
$50? It's worth at least $75.
OK, deal.

▸ 這個多少錢？
那個 100 元。
太貴了，算我 50 元啦。
50 元？這個至少要 75 元。
好，成交。

5
That'll be $52, sir. Cash or credit card?
Credit card, please.

▸ 先生，一共 52 元，請問您要付現還是刷卡？
刷卡。

6 | Hello. I want to return this sweater.
OK. Do you have the receipt?
Yes, here you go. Can I get a refund?
No, I'm sorry. But you can exchange it for another sweater.

▸ 哈囉，我想要退這件毛衣。
好的，請問您有帶發票嗎？
有，在這裡。可以退錢嗎？
很抱歉，沒辦法，但是您可以換其他的毛衣。

Sentence Patterns
(069) p. 49

- 請問盥洗用品在哪裡？
請問冷凍食品／電子產品在哪裡？
在第三走道。
- 你們有賣洗髮精嗎？
很抱歉，賣完了。
- 我可以試這件的其他顏色嗎？
- 你們這個有其他尺寸嗎？
- 您想要試什麼顏色？
藍色。
- 這個／這些多少錢？
20 元。
- 太貴了！
價錢挺公道的！
- 您要如何付款？
我要付現。
- 我要退這雙鞋。
- 這太小了。
這是壞的。
- 我可以退錢嗎？
- 我有發票。

(III) Now, Time to Listen!
p. 50

1 Ⓐ 1 F 2 T 3 F (070)
Ⓑ 1 T 2 T 3 F

Script & Translation

Ⓐ | Lucy | Excuse me. I'm trying to find the toiletries.
| Staff | Toiletries are on aisle seven.
| Lucy | Thank you. Oh, one more question. Do you have any deodorant in stock?
| Staff | Yes, deodorant is on the top shelf.
| 露西 | 不好意思，我要找盥洗用品。
| 店員 | 盥洗用品在第七走道。

| 露西 | 謝謝。噢，還有一個問題。你們有賣體香劑嗎？
| 店員 | 有，體香劑在架子的最上層。

Ⓑ | Staff | That's $32. How do you want to pay today?
| Lucy | With cash, please.
| Staff | OK. No problem.
| Lucy | Oh, I also bought a CD here last week, but it's broken. Can I get a refund?
| Staff | Do you have the receipt?
| Lucy | No, I lost it.
| Staff | I'm sorry, ma'am. We can't give refunds without a receipt.

| 店員 | 一共 32 元，請問您今天要如何付款？
| 露西 | 我要刷卡。
| 店員 | 好的，沒問題。
| 露西 | 噢，還有我上週在這裡買了一片 CD，可是它是壞的，可以退錢嗎？
| 店員 | 請問您有發票嗎？
| 露西 | 沒有，我弄不見了。
| 店員 | 小姐，我很抱歉，但如果沒有發票就無法退錢。

2  1 d 2 b 3 e 4 c 5 a (071)

Script & Translation

1 | A | Excuse me. Do you have these shoes in a bigger size?
| B | No, sorry. These are the biggest ones we have.
| A | 不好意思，這雙鞋有沒有大一點的尺寸？
| B | 抱歉，沒有，這雙是最大號了。

2 | A | I bought these jeans yesterday, but they don't fit me.
| B | Oh, I'm sorry. Do you want to exchange them for another pair?
| A | 我昨天買了這件牛仔褲，可是不合身。
| B | 噢，不好意思。您要換一件嗎？

3 | A | How much are these shoes?
| B | They're $40, sir.
| A | Oh no! That's too expensive. Will you take $20 for them?
| A | 這雙鞋多少錢？
| B | 40 元，先生。
| A | 噢，不！太貴了，算我 20 元可以嗎？

4 | A | Excuse me. I'm looking for men's clothes.
| B | Men's clothes are upstairs, sir.
| A | 不好意思，我在找男裝。
| B | 先生，男裝在樓上。

5 A | Can I pay for these jeans with my credit card?

B | I'm sorry, sir. We only accept cash at this store.

A | 這件牛仔褲可以用刷卡結帳嗎？

B | 很抱歉，先生，我們店裡只收現金。

③

1 How much, reasonable (072)

2 in stock, on aisle, bottom shelf

3 looking for, sold out

4 different size, try, eight

5 bought, receipt, a refund

🎧 Translation

1 A | 不好意思，請問這台 DVD 播放器多少錢？

B | 200 元，因為是最新型的。

A | 喔，其實我覺得這個價錢很合理。

2 A | 不好意思，請問你們有賣牙膏嗎？

B | 有，牙膏應該在第二走道吧。

A | 我找過了，那邊沒有。

B | 噢，在架子的底層，可能不好找。

3 A | 哈囉，我在找蘋果。

B | 不好意思，我們蘋果賣完了。

4 A | 這件衣服很好看，有沒有別的尺寸？

B | 有的，請問您想要試什麼尺寸？

A | 八號。

B | 好的，我現在去幫您拿。

5 A | 我昨天買了這件 T 恤，可是上面有破洞。

B | 噢，對不起，您有帶發票的話，我可以退款給您。

IV Now, Grammar Time! p. 51

④

1 and, but　**2** or, so　**3** or, and

⑤

2 Lucy likes the yellow boots, but she doesn't like the red ones.

3 Tom kept his receipt, so he can get a refund.

4 shampoo, or she can buy toothpaste.

5 Rob doesn't want the jeans, nor does he want the sweater.

6 I had the receipt, yet/but they still didn't give me a refund.

7 I can't show you any different sizes, for we don't have any in stock.

8 Toiletries are on aisle five, and makeup is on aisle six.

V Now, Time to Speak! p. 53

⑥

🎧 Translation (073)

Ⓐ A | 不好意思，我要找眼線筆。

B | 眼線筆在第六走道。

A | 謝謝。

Ⓑ A | 不好意思，我可以試穿這件 T 恤嗎？

B | 當然可以，試穿間在那邊。

A | 這件有點太大了，有別的尺寸嗎？

Ⓒ A | 不好意思，請問這支手錶多少錢？

B | 100 元。

A | 哇！好貴。30 元好不好？

⑧

🎧 Translation (074)

老闆 | 哈囉，有看到您喜歡的嗎？

顧客 | 有，我滿喜歡這個茶壺。

老闆 | 喔，對啊，很美吧？

顧客 | 多少錢？

老闆 | 50 元。

顧客 | 太貴了！

老闆 | 可是這個茶壺有 70 年的歷史喔，先生。

顧客 | 50 元我買不下手，10 元賣不賣？

老闆 | 這至少值 40 元。

顧客 | 好吧，那算我 30 元？

老闆 | 我的底價是 35 元，你看這色澤多美。

顧客 | 好吧，這裡是 35 元，給你。

VI Now, Time to Pronounce! p. 55

⑨

1 knelt　**2** grin　**3** mow (076)

4 sun　**5** mill

⑪ 4, 5, 6, 7, 8, 9, 10 (079)

⑫

1 [n] [ŋ] [m] [n] (080)

2 [m] [n] [n] [ŋ]

3 [n] [ŋ] [n] [ŋ]

4 [n] [n] [m] [ŋ]

I Topic Preview p. 56 〔081〕

1
This is 911. What's your emergency?
My father is having a heart attack.
What's your address?
Twenty-one Pine Avenue.
The paramedics will be there soon.

▸ 這裡是 911，請問您有什麼急事？
我父親心臟病發。
您的地址是？
松蔭大道 21 號。
醫務人員很快就到。

2
This is 911. What's your emergency?
Someone just stole my bag.
Are you hurt?
No, I'm fine. I'm outside number three Oak Boulevard.
We're sending the police now.

▸ 這裡是 911，請問您有什麼急事？
剛剛有人偷了我的包包。
您有沒有受傷？
沒有，我沒事。我在橡樹大道 3 號門外。
我們馬上派警察過去。

3
Hello? Is this 911? My house is on fire.
Stay calm. Are you inside the house now?
No, I'm outside.
Do not go back in. What's your address?
Forty-five Holly Drive.
The fire department is on the way.

▸ 哈囉？請問是 911 嗎？我家失火了。
請別慌張，您現在還在屋內嗎？
我在外面。
請勿回到屋內。您的地址是哪裡？
荷利大道 45 號。
消防隊已經在路上了。

4
Help! Can someone please help me?
What's the problem?
My son is choking!
It's OK. I know the Heimlich maneuver.

▸ 救人啊！有沒有人可以幫幫忙？
怎麼了？
我兒子噎到了。
別擔心，我會哈姆力克急救法。

Sentence Patterns 〔083〕 p. 57

- 請問您有什麼急事？
  請問怎麼了？
  我妹妹溺水了。
  我起過敏反應。
  我被攻擊了。
  有人偷了我的手機。
- 請問您的地址在哪裡？／您在哪裡？
- 保持鎮定。／沒事的。／您有沒有受傷？
- 救護車已經在路上了。
- 這裡有沒有人會急救？
- 這裡有沒有人會用夾板固定斷腿？
- 這裡有沒有人會將肩膀復位？
  這裡有沒有人是醫生？
- 我會急救。／我知道如何清理傷口。
- 請幫幫我！／我需要幫助！／拜託誰來幫幫我？

III Now, Time to Listen! p. 58

1 **1** a, d **2** b, c **3** c **4** a, b, d

Script & Translation

1	911 Operator	This is 911. What's your emergency?
	Woman	My husband is having an allergic reaction.
	911 Operator	To what?
	Woman	He ate a cheese sandwich. He's allergic to cheese.
	911 Operator	Stay calm. The paramedics are on the way.
	911 總機	這裡是 911，請問您有什麼急事？
	女子	我丈夫起了過敏反應。
	911 總機	什麼樣的過敏？
	女子	他吃了一個起司三明治，他對起司過敏。
	911 總機	您先保持冷靜，醫務人員已經出發了。
2	Man	Hello? Is this 911?
	911 Operator	Yes, this is 911. What's your emergency?
	Man	I was just attacked on the street.
	911 Operator	Are you hurt?
	Man	Yes, I think my arm is broken.
	911 Operator	Stay where you are. An ambulance and the police will be there soon.

男子	喂，911 嗎？
911 總機	是的，這裡是 911，請問您有什麼急事？
男子	我剛才在路上被攻擊了。
911 總機	您有沒有受傷？
男子	有，我的手臂好像斷了。
911 總機	請待在原地，救護車和警察馬上過去。

3

Man	Fire! Help! My house is on fire!
911 Operator	OK sir, stay calm. What's your address?
Man	Eighty-nine Beech Drive. Please hurry. My cat is still in the house!
911 Operator	The fire department is on the way. Sir, please stay outside. Do not go back into the house.

男子	失火了！救命！我家失火了！
911 總機	好的，先生，您先冷靜。您的地址是？
男子	山毛櫸道 89 號。請快一點，我的貓還在屋子裡！
911 總機	消防隊已經出發了。先生，請留在屋外，不要回到屋內。

4

911 Operator	This is 911. What's your emergency?
Woman	I've lost my keys. I can't find them.
911 Operator	Ma'am, 911 is an emergency number. We can't help you with this problem.
Woman	But I have to leave the house right now!
911 Operator	Nine-one-one is for real emergencies only. I'm sorry.

911 總機	這裡是 911，請問您有什麼急事？
女子	我的鑰匙不見了，我找不到。
911 總機	小姐，911 是緊急救助電話，這個狀況我們幫不上忙。
女子	可是我現在一定要出門！
911 總機	真正的緊急事件才能打 911，很抱歉。

2   1 – 8 – 3 – 9 – 4 – 5 – 6 – 2 – 7   （086）

Script & Translation

911 Operator	Nine-one-one. What's your emergency?
Woman	Help! Someone's in my house! I think it's a burglar.

911 Operator	OK. Stay calm. What's your address?
Woman	It's 53 North Road. Please, send the police quickly.
911 Operator	The police are on their way. Are you in your bedroom?
Woman	Yes, I am. The burglar is downstairs in the living room.
911 Operator	Stay in your bedroom. Can you lock the door?
Woman	Yes. What should I do now?
911 Operator	Stay on the phone. The police will be there in two minutes.

911 總機	這裡是 911，請問您有什麼急事？
女子	救命！有人闖進我家！我覺得是竊賊。
911 總機	好，先別慌，您的地址在哪裡？
女子	北方路 53 號，拜託你們快派警察過來。
911 總機	警察已經動身前往，您在房間內嗎？
女子	對。竊賊在樓下的客廳裡。
911 總機	您待在房間別出去，門可以鎖嗎？
女子	可以，我現在該怎麼辦？
911 總機	我們保持通話，警察過兩分鐘就到。

3   1 b 2 e 3 a 4 d 5 c   （087）

Script & Translation

1 Help! I cut my leg. Does anyone here know first aid?
救命！我的腿割傷了，這裡有人會急救嗎？

2 Hello, is this 911?
喂，請問是 911 嗎？

3 My father just had a heart attack! Can someone help?
我父親剛才心臟病發！有人能幫忙嗎？

4 I was in a car accident. I'm hurt badly.
我出了車禍，傷得很嚴重。

5 Ouch! I think I just dislocated my shoulder!
唉喲！我的肩膀好像脫臼了！

IV Now, Grammar Time!   p. 60

4
2 looks like, feels
3 sounds like / seems like / looks like
4 smells, smells like
5 feels / seems, sounds

5
- a feels, hot
- b looks, red
- c sounds like, being attacked
- d smells like, burning
- e looks like, drowning
- f seems like, a cold

V Now, Time to Speak! p. 62

7

Translation 〔088〕

A 誰能幫幫忙？我朋友昏倒了！
B 別擔心，我會急救，我可以幫忙。
A 他會不會有事？
B 他一會兒就會沒事的。／立刻打 911！

VI Now, Time to Pronounce! p. 65

8
| 1 wire | 2 lip | 3 roam | 〔090〕 |
| 4 red | 5 load | | |

| 1 [l] | 2 [l] | 3 [r] | 〔091〕 |
| 4 [r] | 5 [l] | | |

Script

1 lice 2 latte 3 read 4 rift 5 wild

Unit 08

I Topic Preview p. 66 〔094〕

✱ *Formal* 正式

1
> Hello. ABC Firm. How may I help you?
> Hello. This is Jasmine White from XYZ Firm. May I speak to Mike Powers, please?
> This is he.
> I'm calling in regards to the email I received from you.

▸ 喂，ABC 公司，您好，請問有什麼可以為您服務的地方？
喂，我是 XYZ 公司的嘉絲敏・懷特，我要找麥克・鮑爾斯。
我就是。
我是打來跟你談你寄來的 email。

2
> Hello. Is this Mike Powers?
> I'm sorry. I think you have the wrong number.

▸ 喂，請問是麥克・鮑爾斯嗎？
不好意思，你打錯電話了。

3
> Thank you very much for your time. Goodbye.

▸ 謝謝您花時間與我交談，再見。

✱ *Informal* 非正式

1
> Hello. Mike here.
> Hi, Mike. It's Jasmine.
> Oh, hi, Jasmine. What's up?
> I'm just calling to see if you have free time later.

▸ 哈囉，我是麥克。
嗨，麥克，我是嘉絲敏。
喔，嗨，嘉絲敏，什麼事？
我只是打來問你等一下有沒有空。

2
> Hello. Can you hear me?
> I'm sorry. You're breaking up. The signal is very bad.

▸ 喂，你聽得到我說話嗎？
不好意思，你的聲音斷斷續續的，收訊很差。

3
> Talk to you later. Bye.

▸ 再聊喔，掰。

Sentence Patterns 〔096〕 p. 67

- 我是傑克・懷特。
  我就是傑克・懷特。
  嗨，我是傑克。
- 請問哪裡可以為您服務？
  請找瑪麗・鮑爾斯。
  瑪麗在嗎？
  你是瑪麗嗎？
  我就是。
- 請您稍等。
  稍等。
  我幫您轉接。
- 我打來詢問面試的事。
  我打來討論您的訂單。
  我打來跟你說我會晚點到。
  我打來安排會議。
- 可以請您幫我留言嗎？
  請問您要留言嗎？
- 很抱歉，你打錯電話了。
- 我聽不見你的聲音，訊號很差。
  你的聲音斷斷續續的。
- 謝謝你花時間與我交談。
  感謝您的來電。
  下次再聊。

Ⅲ Now, Time to Listen!

p. 68

1 **A** **1** a **2** b **3** a （097）

   B **1** c **2** a **3** c （098）

Script & Translation

A

Sharon Jones	Hello. Sharon Jones speaking.
David Price	Hello, Ms. Jones. This is David Price. I'm calling about my interview tomorrow. I'm sorry, but I don't think I can make it. Can we perhaps reschedule?
Sharon Jones	OK, Mr. Price. Let me transfer you to my secretary, and maybe she can arrange another date. Let me put you on hold for a second.
David Price	Thank you so much. I'm so sorry for the inconvenience.
雪倫・瓊斯	喂，我是雪倫・瓊斯。
大衛・普萊斯	喂，瓊斯女士，我是大衛・普萊斯，我打電話來是為了明天面試的事情。很抱歉，我可能沒辦法過去，能否改期呢？
雪倫・瓊斯	好的，普萊斯先生，我把電話轉過去給我秘書，她或許可以安排其他時間，請您稍等。
大衛・普萊斯	非常感謝您，很抱歉讓您麻煩了。

B

Joe	Hello. Joe speaking.
Maria	Hello, Joe. It's Maria.
Joe	Oh, hi, Maria! How are you?
Maria	I'm good, thanks. You?
Joe	Yeah, I'm good. What's up?
Maria	I'm just calling to see if you want to go for dinner this Friday.
Joe	Sure. I've got some free time on Friday. What time?
Maria	Around eight? I'll call a restaurant to make a reservation.
Joe	Great. Call me with the details.
Maria	OK. Talk to you soon.
Joe	Bye!

喬	喂，我是喬。
瑪麗亞	喂，喬，我是瑪麗亞。
喬	喔，嗨，瑪麗亞！你好嗎？
瑪麗亞	我很好，謝謝。你呢？
喬	我很好，有什麼事嗎？
瑪麗亞	我只是打來問你，這個星期五要不要一起吃晚餐？
喬	好啊，我星期五有空，幾點？
瑪麗亞	大概八點可以嗎？我先打電話去餐廳訂位。
喬	好，再打電話跟我說細節。
瑪麗亞	好，我再跟你說。
喬	掰！

2 **1** d - 2 **2** c - 4 **3** a - 3 **4** b - 1 （099）

Script & Translation

1

Janet	Hello. Peartree Publishers. How may I help you?
Matt	Hello. Is that Janet?
Janet	This is she.
Matt	Hi, Janet. It's Matt. I'm feeling sick today, so I won't be coming into work.
Janet	Oh, hi, Matt. OK. I'll tell the boss.
珍妮特	喂，梨樹出版社，您好。請問有什麼可以為您服務的地方？
麥特	喂，珍妮特嗎？
珍妮特	我就是。
麥特	嗨，珍妮特，我是麥特。我今天身體不舒服，所以不會去上班。
珍妮特	喔，嗨，麥特。好，我會轉告老闆。

2

Woman	Hello. Reception desk.
Matt	Hi. I'm in room 216, and there's a problem with my room.
Woman	I'm sorry to hear that, sir. What seems to be the problem?
Matt	The room is too small.
Woman	OK. We'll arrange a new room for you and call you when it's ready.
Matt	Thank you very much.
女士	喂，接待櫃檯，您好。
麥特	嗨，我這裡是 216 號房，我的房間有點問題。
女士	非常抱歉，先生。請問是什麼問題？
麥特	這個房間太小了。
女士	好的，我們會幫您安排新的房間，等整理好就通知您。
麥特	非常感謝。

3	Woman	Hello. Sainsberry Supermarket.
	Matt	Hello. May I speak to the store manager, please?
	Woman	This is she. How can I help you?
	Matt	Oh, hello. This is Matt Baker. I'm calling in regards to your email. It said to call you to arrange an interview.
	Woman	Yes, Matt, hello. Can you come in this Friday at 2:00 p.m.?
	Matt	Yes, no problem.
	Woman	OK great. It was nice speaking to you. See you this Friday.
	Matt	OK. Thanks for your time. Bye.
	女士	喂，森寶利超市，您好。
	麥特	喂，請找店經理。
	女士	我就是，請問有什麼能為您服務？
	麥特	喔，哈囉。我是麥特·貝克，打電話給您是關於您寄來的 email，上面說可以來電安排面試。
	女士	是的，麥特，哈囉。你可以在本週五下午兩點過來嗎？
	麥特	可以，沒問題。
	女士	那太好了，很高興與您交談，那麼這個星期五見了。
	麥特	好的，謝謝您的寶貴時間，再見。
4	Nurse	Hello, Wellness Clinic. How may I help you?
	Matt	Hi, I'm calling to make an appointment with Doctor Wang.
	Nurse	OK. Doctor Wang actually has a space this afternoon.
	Matt	Oh, great. What time?
	Nurse	At 3:30.
	Matt	That's perfect.
	Nurse	Can I get your full name, please?
	Matt	Matt Baker.
	Nurse	Thank you, Mr. Baker. See you this afternoon.
	護士	喂，健康診所，您好。請問有什麼可以為您服務？
	麥特	嗨，我是打來預約王醫師的門診。
	護士	好的，其實王醫師今天下午有空。
	麥特	喔，真好，幾點？
	護士	三點半。
	麥特	太好了。
	護士	請問您貴姓大名？
	麥特	麥特·貝克。
	護士	謝謝，貝克先生，下午見。

3 ❶ F ❷ T ❸ T ❹ F ❺ F (100)

Script & Translation

Secretary	Hello, Woodstock Paper Company. How may I help you?
Sam	Hello. May I speak to Jo Bennett, please? It's Sam Black from Peartree Publishing.
Secretary	I'm sorry. Ms. Bennett's out for lunch at the moment. Can you call back later?
Sam	That's OK. Can I leave a message, then?
Secretary	Of course.
Sam	Tell her that I need to reschedule our meeting to 2:30 p.m. on Tuesday.
Secretary	OK. I'll give her the message when she gets back. Anything else?
Sam	Oh, yes. Can you tell her that the order we placed last week is late?
Secretary	OK, I'll let her know.
Sam	Thanks. Tell her to call me back this afternoon.
Secretary	No problem.
Sam	OK, thank you very much. Bye.
Secretary	Goodbye.
秘書	喂，木緣紙業，您好。請問有什麼能為您服務？
山姆	喂，請找喬·班尼特。我是梨樹出版社的山姆·布萊克。
秘書	很抱歉，班尼特小姐目前外出吃午餐，可以麻煩您晚點再來電嗎？
山姆	沒關係，那我可以留言嗎？
秘書	當然可以。
山姆	請轉告她，我要把會面時間改為星期二下午兩點半。
秘書	好的，她一回來我就轉告她。還有其他事嗎？
山姆	喔，有。請告訴她，我們上週訂的品項延遲了。
秘書	好的，我會轉告她。
山姆	謝謝，請她今天下午回電給我。
秘書	沒問題。
山姆	好，非常感謝你，掰。
秘書	再見。

IV Now, Grammar Time! p. 70

4
❶ waiting	❷ to leave
❸ to speak	❹ to call / calling
❺ to transfer	❻ to put
❼ to reschedule	❽ making
❾ to take / taking	❿ discussing

5
2 to place an order
3 to invite you
4 to make an appointment
5 to reschedule our meeting

V Now, Time to Speak! p. 72

6

Translation Sample Answers

1 A Hello. Thank you for calling Microspot Computer Company. How may I help you?

B <u>Hello. This is Gina Wang from Everest Culture Ltd. May I speak to Bill Grates, please?</u>

A Yes. I'll transfer your call. <u>Let me put you on hold for a minute.</u>

A 喂，微點電腦公司，感謝您的來電。請問有哪裡可以為您服務？

B 喂，我是艾弗勒斯文化有限公司的王吉娜，我要找比爾・葛瑞茲。

A 好的，我幫您轉接，<u>請您稍候</u>。

2 A Hello. James speaking.

B <u>Hi, James. Paul here.</u>

A Oh, hi, Paul! <u>What's up?</u>

B I'm <u>just calling to ask if you want to have dinner later.</u>

A Sure. Sounds good. Call me later with the details.

B OK. <u>Talk to you later.</u>

A Bye.

A 喂，我是詹姆斯。

B 嗨，詹姆斯，我是保羅。

A 喔，嗨，保羅！什麼事？

B 只是打來問你等一下要不要一起吃晚餐？

A 好啊，不錯啊。那你等一下再打來跟我說詳細時間地點。

B 好，一會兒跟你說。

A 掰。

3 A Hello?

B Hello. Is this John?

A No, <u>I'm sorry. You have the wrong number.</u>

B Oh, <u>sorry to bother you.</u>

A 喂？

B 喂，約翰嗎？

A 不是，<u>不好意思，你打錯電話了。</u>

B 噢，<u>對不起打擾了。</u>

VI Now, Time to Pronounce! p. 73

8 1 meat 2 ship 3 grit 🎧102
4 weep 5 leap

[i] eat, eels, sea, We, beach 🎧103
[ɪ] sit, in, winter

Unit 09

I Topic Preview p. 74

1 Could you do me a favor?
Sure. What is it?
Could you lend me some money?
[willing] OK. How much do you need?
[unwilling] Sorry, I'm broke.

▸ 你可以幫我一個忙嗎？
好啊，什麼事？
可以借我錢嗎？
【願意】可以啊，你需要多少錢？
【不願意】很抱歉，我破產了。

2 Excuse me. Could you help me with something?
Oh, I'm sorry. I'm busy at the moment.
It'll just take a second. I'd be ever so grateful.
OK. What do you need?
Could you hold my coffee for a minute?

▸ 不好意思，你可以幫我一下嗎？
噢，不好意思，我正在忙。
只要一下就好了，感激不盡。
好吧，你要我幫什麼忙？
可以幫我拿一下這杯咖啡嗎？

3 Do you mind if I use your phone to go online?
[willing] No, not at all.
[unwilling] Sorry. My phone's not working.

▸ 你介不介意我用你的手機上網？
【願意】一點也不介意啊。
【不願意】不好意思，我的手機壞掉了。

4 Excuse me. Could I get some more ketchup?
Sure. I'll take care of it for you right away.
And could I get another coke, too?
Sure. I'll be right back.

19

▶ 不好意思，可以再給我一點番茄醬嗎？
好的，我馬上拿給您。
順便再給我一杯可樂好嗎？
好的，馬上來。

Sentence Patterns (106) p. 75

Asking for a favor 請求協助 ▶

可以借我你的傘嗎？

Asking for permission 徵求許可 ▶

可以借我用你的手機嗎？

Asking for more 索取更多物品 ▶

可以再給我一杯咖啡嗎？
可以再給我一個盤子嗎？
能不能再給我一些叉子？
再給我一些水好嗎？

III Now, Time to Listen! p. 76

1 1 4 2 1 3 3 4 2 5 5 (107)

🎧 Script & Translation

	Grace	Hi, Paul. Could you do me a favor? I'm going on vacation next week. Would you mind . . .
1	葛瑞絲	嗨，保羅，你可以幫我一個忙嗎？我下週要去度假，你能不能……
2	Grace	Paul, could you do me a favor? I don't have time to go out and buy lunch. Could you . . .
	葛瑞絲	保羅，你可以幫我一個忙嗎？我沒有時間出去買午餐，你可不可以……
3	Grace	Hey, Paul. Sorry to bother you. I just missed the bus home. Could you . . .
	葛瑞絲	嘿，保羅，不好意思打擾一下，我錯過了回家的公車，你可不可以……
4	Grace	Mmm. That was delicious. Oh no! I forgot to bring my wallet. Sorry, Paul. Would you mind . . .
	葛瑞絲	嗯，好好吃喔。噢，不！我忘了帶皮夾，對不起，保羅，你可不可以……
5	Grace	Hi, Paul. Can I ask you a favor? I lost my keys and can't get into my house. Do you mind if I . . .
	葛瑞絲	嗨，保羅，可以請你幫忙嗎？我的鑰匙不見了，進不去我家，你介不介意讓我……

🎧 Script & Translation

	Grace	Hi, Paul. Could you do me a favor? I'm going on vacation next week. Would you mind feeding my cat while I'm away?
1	Paul	Sorry, Grace. I'm actually allergic to cats.
	葛瑞絲	嗨，保羅，你可以幫我一個忙嗎？我下週要去度假，我不在的時候，你能不能幫我餵貓？
	保羅	很抱歉，葛瑞絲，我其實對貓過敏。
2	Grace	Paul, could you do me a favor? I don't have time to go out and buy lunch. Could you get me something from the supermarket?
	Paul	Sure. What do you want? Is a sandwich OK?
	葛瑞絲	保羅，你可以幫我一個忙嗎？我沒有時間出去買午餐，你可不可以幫我去超市買一些東西？
	保羅	好啊，你要什麼？一個三明治可以嗎？
3	Grace	Hey, Paul. Sorry to bother you. I just missed the bus home. Could you give me a ride?
	Paul	Yeah, no problem. Hop in.
	葛瑞絲	嘿，保羅，不好意思打擾一下，我錯過了回家的公車，你可不可以載我？
	保羅	可以啊，沒問題，上車吧。
4	Grace	Mmm. That was delicious. Oh no! I forgot to bring my wallet. Sorry, Paul. Would you mind picking up the check this time?
	Paul	OK, but this is the last time. You do this too often.
	葛瑞絲	嗯，好好吃喔。噢，不！我忘了帶皮夾，對不起，保羅，你可不可以幫我付這次的錢？
	保羅	好，但是下不為例，你老是這樣。
5	Grace	Hi, Paul. Can I ask you a favor? I lost my keys and can't get into my house. Do you mind if I stay at your house tonight?
	Paul	Oh, sorry, Grace. My mom is staying with me at the moment. There's no room I'm afraid.
	葛瑞絲	嗨，保羅，可以請你幫忙嗎？我的鑰匙不見了，進不去我家，你介不介意讓我今晚住你家？

保羅 | 噢，很抱歉，葛瑞絲。我媽現在住在我家，可能沒有位置了。

2

1 Could you, watching my stuff, I can't (109)
   ⓐ two strangers   ⓑ café

2 do me a favor, help me move, no problem
   ⓐ willing   ⓑ knows the man well

3 do you mind / No, not at all / pick up the bill
   ⓐ lets   ⓑ doesn't have

🎧 Translation

1 男 | 不好意思，很抱歉打擾你，可以幫我一下嗎？
  女 | 可以。
  男 | 我想去一下洗手間，可以幫我顧一下我的東西嗎？
  女 | 噢，對不起，沒有辦法，因為我差不多要離開了。

2 女 | 嗨，詹姆斯，不知道你能不能幫我一個忙？
  男 | 我盡量，什麼事？
  女 | 我下個星期要搬家，你能不能幫我搬家？
  男 | 好啊，沒問題。

3 男 | 外面在下雨，裘，你介不介意我用你的電話叫計程車？
  女 | 不會，一點也不介意，電話給你。喔，但是可不可以幫我一個忙？
  男 | 沒問題，儘管說。
  女 | 午餐讓你請好不好？我只剩下一點錢了。

Ⓥ Now, Grammar Time! p. 77

3

2 Could, Would   3 Would
4 can, will, could, would
5 Would   6 Could, May
7 could, should   8 Would
9 Can, Shall   10 will

4

Sample Answers

ⓐ Could I stay at your house tonight? / Would you mind if I stayed at your house tonight?

ⓑ I'll get you some more. / Shall I get you some more? / Would you like some more?

ⓒ Can/Shall I get you something to eat? Can/Could I get a sandwich?

ⓓ Can/Will/Could you do me a favor? Can/Will/Could you get me something from 7-11?

Ⓒ Translation

ⓐ A | 我今晚可以在你家過夜嗎？／你介不介意我今晚住你家？
  B | 好啊，沒問題，你可以睡沙發。

ⓑ A | 噢，不！那是最後一塊蛋糕嗎？太好吃了。
  B | 我再拿一些給你。／要不要我再拿一些給你？／你想再吃一些嗎？廚房裡還有一個蛋糕。

ⓒ A | 你好像很餓的樣子，要不要我弄東西給你吃？
  B | 我可以吃一個三明治嗎？謝謝媽媽。

ⓓ A | 嘿，你可以幫我一個忙嗎？
  B | 可以啊，你需要我幫你什麼？
  A | 我沒有時間出去吃午餐，你可以去 7-11 幫我買點東西嗎？

Ⓥ Now, Time to Speak! p. 79

6

🎧 Translation (110)

顧客 | 不好意思，可以再給我一支叉子嗎？這支掉到地上了。
服務生 | 沒問題，我馬上拿來。還需要別的嗎？
顧客 | 再給我一點鹽好嗎？
服務生 | 好的，馬上來。

Ⓥ Now, Time to Pronounce! p. 81

8

1 [ɛ] [e]   (112)
2 [ɛ] [e] [e]
3 [ɛ] [e] [ɛ] [e]
4 [ɛ] [e] [e] [ɛ] [ɛ]

9

[e] 2, 4, 5, 8   [ɛ] 1, 3, 6, 7   (113)

Unit 10

Ⓘ Topic Preview p. 82 (114)

1 | Ooo . . . I'm not feeling too well.
  What's wrong?
  I feel like I'm going to be sick.
  Sit down and drink some water.
  -
  Are you OK? You look terrible.
  Ooo . . . I feel really ill.
  Do you want to go and lie down?
  Yes, I think I will.

▸ 嗚……我不太舒服。
怎麼了？
我好像快要生病了。
坐下來喝點水。

你還好嗎？你臉色看起來很差。
嗚……我很不舒服。
你要不要去躺一下？
好，我會的。

2
What seems to be the problem?
I have a runny nose and I'm always shivering.
OK, anything else?
I have a rash on my stomach.

▸ 你哪邊不舒服？
我流鼻水，而且一直發抖。
好，還有嗎？
肚子這邊長疹子。

3
Doctor, I have a really bad headache.
Do you watch a lot of TV?
Yes, I watch TV until late at night.
You should watch less TV.

Doctor, I can't get to sleep.
Take these sleeping pills.

▸ 醫生，我的頭很痛。
你看很多電視嗎？
對，我晚上看電視看到很晚。
你應該少看一點電視。

醫生，我睡不著。
吃這些安眠藥。

4
I don't think I can come in to work today.
Oh, why not?
I'm feeling really ill. I have a terrible stomachache.
What did the doctor say?
He told me to stay home and rest.

▸ 我想我今天不能去上班了。
噢，為什麼？
我很不舒服，肚子很痛。
醫生怎麼說？
他要我在家裡休息。

Sentence Patterns

(116) p. 83

• 怎麼了？
發生什麼事？
你還好嗎？
你看起來很不舒服。
我不舒服。／我不太舒服。／我覺得不舒服。

• 我流鼻水。
我發高燒。
我的頭一直昏昏的。
我喉嚨痛。
我眼睛癢。
• 你覺得噁心想吐嗎？
你有沒有頭昏或發燒？
• 你應該是胃部感染。
你應該是感冒了。
• 你喝很多咖啡嗎？
你看很多電視嗎？
• 你要多喝點水。
你要少看一點電視。
• 休息幾天。
不要抓它！
吃這些藥。
• 醫生要我吃藥和休息。

III Now, Time to Listen!
p. 84

1

2	Symptoms	Illness
	• feels dizzy	the flu
	• fever	

(117)

3	Symptoms	Advice
	• insomnia	• rest
	• rash	• don't scratch the rash

4	Symptoms	Illness	Advice
	• left ear hurts	ear infection	• put medicine in ear
	• headache		

Script & Translation

1	Jamie	Ooo . . . Doctor, I feel really ill.
	Doctor	Can you tell me some of your symptoms?
	Jamie	I have a really bad stomachache, and I feel nauseous all the time.
	Doctor	It's probably a stomach infection.
	Jamie	What should I do?
	Doctor	Take this medicine and don't eat any oily food.
	潔咪	嗚……醫生，我好不舒服。
	醫生	把症狀跟我說好嗎？
	潔咪	肚子痛得很厲害，而且我一直想吐。
	醫生	可能是胃部感染。
	潔咪	那我該怎麼辦？
	醫生	吃這種藥，不要吃油膩的食物。

2 Zara | Doctor, I feel dizzy all the time. What's wrong with me?
Doctor | Do you have a runny nose or a fever?
Zara | Yeah, I have a fever.
Doctor | I think you have the flu. Stay at home and drink lots of water.

薩拉 | 醫生，我一直頭昏，我怎麼了？
醫生 | 有沒有流鼻水或發燒？
薩拉 | 有，我有發燒。
醫生 | 那應該是流感，在家休息，多喝點水。

3 Doctor | What seems to be the problem?
Kayla | I can't sleep and I have this rash on my back.
Doctor | Hmm, insomnia and a rash. I'm not sure. Have you been on vacation recently?
Kayla | Yes, I went to Africa last month.
Doctor | I see. I think you might have a rare disease.
Kayla | Oh no! What should I do?
Doctor | Don't worry. We'll do some tests. But right now, you should go home and rest, and don't scratch the rash.

醫生 | 怎麼了？
凱拉 | 我失眠，而且背部長了這樣的疹子。
醫生 | 嗯，失眠和疹子，我還不能確定是什麼問題。你最近有出去度假嗎？
凱拉 | 有，我上個月去非洲。
醫生 | 了解，你可能得了少見的疾病。
凱拉 | 噢，不！那我該怎麼辦？
醫生 | 別擔心，我們會做一些檢驗。現在你先回家休息，不要去抓疹子。

4 Mia | Hello, doctor. My left ear hurts a lot.
Doctor | Do you have any problems hearing?
Mia | Yes, I can't hear very well.
Doctor | OK, let me see. Hmm. Do you have a headache?
Mia | Yes, a really bad one.
Doctor | Well, it looks like you have an ear infection.
Mia | OK. What should I do?
Doctor | Just put this medicine in your ear and it should be OK after about a week.

米雅 | 哈囉，醫生。我的左耳很痛。
醫生 | 聽力有沒有問題呢？

米雅 | 有，聽不太清楚。
醫生 | 好，我看看。嗯，會不會頭痛？
米雅 | 會，很痛。
醫生 | 好，看起來是耳部感染。
米雅 | 喔，那怎麼辦？
醫生 | 點這種耳藥，大概一個禮拜就會好了。

2 **a** 2 **b** 5 **c** 1 **d** 4 **e** 3 (118)

Script & Translation

Jack | Hello, Boss? This is Jack.
Boss | Hey, Jack. Is everything OK?
Jack | Not really. I don't feel very well today. I think I need to take a day off.
Boss | Oh, what's the matter?
Jack | I have a really bad stomachache, and I feel dizzy.
Boss | Gosh, have you been to see the doctor?
Jack | Yeah, I went yesterday. He said it might be a rare stomach disease.
Boss | Oh no! That sounds serious.
Jack | Yeah. It hurts so much. I didn't even eat breakfast this morning.
Boss | OK. No problem, Jack. You stay home and get plenty of rest.
Jack | Thanks, Boss. Bye.

傑克 | 喂，老闆，我是傑克。
老闆 | 嘿，傑克，還好嗎？
傑克 | 不太好，我今天不太舒服，可能必須請一天假。
老闆 | 噢，怎麼了？
傑克 | 肚子很痛，頭又昏。
老闆 | 唉呀！你有沒有去看醫生？
傑克 | 有，昨天去了。他說可能是罕見的胃疾。
老闆 | 噢，不會吧！聽起來很嚴重。
傑克 | 對啊，好痛。我今天早上連早餐都沒吃。
老闆 | 好，沒問題的，傑克，你在家好好休息。
傑克 | 謝謝老闆，再見。

3 **1** sore throat, cough **c** (119)
2 have, eczema **e**
3 fever, rash **d**
4 feel nauseous, eat **a**
5 head hurts, muscle pain **b**

Translation

1 病人 | 我的喉嚨痛，而且咳個不停。
醫生 | 你要用鹽水漱口，並且多喝溫水。
2 病人 | 我背上的濕疹很嚴重。
醫生 | 一天擦兩次這種藥膏，盡量先趴著睡。

3 病人　我發燒，而且手臂上長疹子。
　　醫生　你要在額頭上冰敷，如果開始癢的話，就擦這種藥膏。

4 病人　我很想吐，什麼都吃不下。
　　醫生　喝一點熱湯，休息一下。

5 病人　我頭痛，肌肉也痠痛得厲害。
　　醫生　吃這些止痛藥，它們對各種疼痛都很有效。

IV Now, Grammar Time!
p. 86

4
2 My arm doesn't hurt.
3 The rash doesn't itch.
4 I didn't take a sleeping pill last night.
5 I don't have a rare disease.
6 The doctor didn't give me medicine.

5
2 Do you have a fever, too?
Do you think it's the flu?
3 What medicine did you take?
How many did you take?
4 Why do you need sleeping pills?
5 Why do you think that?
Does it itch?

V Now, Time to Speak!
p. 87

6
🎧 Translation　120

A 醫生　哈囉，怎麼了？
　　病人　我流鼻水和喉嚨痛。
　　醫生　好，應該只是感冒。
　　病人　那要怎麼辦？
　　醫生　多喝水，休息一下。

B 吉姆　喂，老闆嗎？我是吉姆。
　　老闆　吉姆，你的聲音聽起來很糟，你還好嗎？
　　吉姆　不太好，我很不舒服。
　　老闆　怎麼回事？
　　吉姆　我的四肢長了奇怪的疹子，而且一直咳嗽。
　　老闆　醫生怎麼說？
　　吉姆　他說是少見的疾病。他要我休息幾天，並且吃藥。
　　老闆　好的，吉姆，祝你早日康復。

VI Now, Time to Pronounce!
p. 89

10 [æ] family, cat, passing, Matt　122
　　[ɑ] father, mop, Stop, palm

11 1 [ɑ]　2 [ɑ]　3 [æ]　123
　　4 [æ]　5 [ɑ]

🎧 Script
1 farm　2 cart　3 fatter　4 last　5 charm

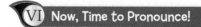

Unit 11

I Topic Preview
p. 90　124

1
I'm really good at basketball.
Oh, yeah? How good.
I can slam-dunk from the three-point line.
Wow, that's impressive!
I play on the college team, too.

▸ 我很會打籃球喔。
喔，是嗎？有多厲害？
我可以從三分線灌籃。
哇，好厲害！
我也是大學校隊喔。

2
Do you play any sports?
Yes, I play soccer quite often.
How often?
Oh, about once a week. You?
I don't play any sports, but I watch a lot on TV.

▸ 你會任何運動嗎？
會啊，我經常踢足球。
多常？
喔，大概一週一次。你呢？
我不太運動，但是我常常看電視轉播。

3
I can play the violin.
Oh really? I didn't know that!
I can do magic, too.
You're full of surprises! Show me!

▸ 我會拉小提琴。
喔，真的嗎？我都不知道！
我還會變魔術。
你真是讓人意料不到耶！變給我看！

4
Do you have any bad habits?
Yes, but I don't want to say.

I'll tell you mine if you tell me yours.
OK. I pick my nose sometimes.
Gross! I bite my nails.
That's not too bad.

▸ 你有什麼壞習慣嗎？
有啊，但是我不想說。
如果你跟我說你的，我就說我的。
好吧，我偶爾會挖鼻孔。
好噁喔！我會咬指甲。
那還好啊。

Sentence Patterns 126 p. 91

- 你的籃球打得好不好？
  我打得很好。
  開什麼玩笑？我很強耶。
- 我很會打網球，我有參加校隊。
- 我每次都發愛司球。
- 好厲害，真想不到耶！
- 我固定練拳擊。／我每週游泳兩次。
- 你有什麼不為人知的才能嗎？
  你最拿手的派對把戲是什麼？
  我會後空翻。
- 噢！我都不知道你會變魔術！
- 你有沒有壞習慣？
  你的壞習慣是什麼？
  我偶爾會抽菸。

III Now, Time to Listen! p. 92

1 **1** a   **2** a   **3** c   127

Script & Translation

Simon	Do you play any sports, Sue?
Sue	Yeah, I play hockey quite often.
Simon	Oh, I play hockey, too. How often do you play?
Sue	About once a week. How about you, Simon?
Simon	Yeah, about the same. Are you any good?
Sue	I'm pretty good. I play on the company team at work. I play soccer now and then, too. But I like hockey more.
賽門	蘇，你會任何運動嗎？
蘇	會，我常常打曲棍球。
賽門	喔，我也會打耶。你多久打一次？

蘇	大概一週一次，你呢，賽門？
賽門	嗯，差不多跟你一樣。你打得很好嗎？
蘇	我滿強的，我在上班的地方有加入公司球隊喔。有時候我也會踢足球，不過我還是比較喜歡曲棍球。

a, b, e 128

Script & Translation

Simon	Well, my favorite sport is baseball.
Sue	I like to watch baseball on TV sometimes.
Simon	You should come and watch me play.
Sue	Really? Are you any good at it?
Simon	Are you kidding? I hit a home run every game.
Sue	Wow, that's impressive!
賽門	喔，我最愛的運動是棒球。
蘇	有時候我也愛看電視棒球轉播。
賽門	你應該來看我打球。
蘇	真的嗎？你打得很好嗎？
賽門	開什麼玩笑？我每場比賽都會擊出全壘打。
蘇	哇，好強喔！

2 a Diana   b Andy   129
  c Matt   d Diana

1 make cocktails   130
2 know you can
3 full of surprises
4 very impressive

Script & Translation

Diana	Matt, can you do magic? I need someone to do some tricks at a dinner party I'm planning.
Matt	Sorry, Diana. I can't. I can make cocktails, though. Do you need a bartender?
Diana	No. I'm going to cook a three-course meal, so we're going to drink wine, not cocktails.
Matt	Oh, I didn't know you can cook.
Diana	Of course. I can cook quite well. I can play the piano, too. Did you know that? I'm going to play at the party.
Matt	Well, you are full of surprises. Oh, hang on. One of my friends can do magic. His name's Andy. I'll call him.
Diana	Does he have any special tricks?
Matt	He can saw a person in half.
Diana	Wow! That's very impressive. Call him right now!

黛安娜	麥特，你會變魔術嗎？我正在策劃一個晚宴，需要會表演變魔術的人。
麥特	不好意思，黛安娜，我不會。可是我會調雞尾酒，你們需要酒保嗎？
黛安娜	不需要，因為我要煮三道菜的大餐，所以我們會喝葡萄酒，不喝雞尾酒。
麥特	哦，我不知道你會做菜耶。
黛安娜	當然會啊，我滿會煮的喔。我也會彈鋼琴，你知道嗎？我會在晚會上表演喔。
麥特	嗯，真想不到耶。喔，等等，我有一個朋友會變魔術，他叫安迪，我可以打電話給他。
黛安娜	他會變什麼特別的魔術嗎？
麥特	他可以把人鋸成兩半。
黛安娜	哇！太厲害了，現在就打給他！

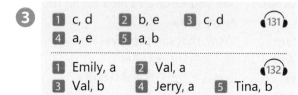

3

1 c, d	2 b, e	3 c, d	(131)
4 a, e	5 a, b		

1 Emily, a	2 Val, a	(132)
3 Val, b	4 Jerry, a	5 Tina, b

Script & Translation

1 Hi. I'm Jerry. My bad habit is snoring. I snore every night. I also smoke sometimes, but only about twice a week.

嗨，我是傑瑞。我的壞習慣是打鼾，我每天晚上都會打鼾。我偶爾也會抽菸，但一週大約只抽兩次。

2 I'm Val, and my bad habit is procrastinating. I love to waste time. I procrastinate at least 10 times a day! I also bite my nails a lot, too—about once an hour.

我是瓦爾，我的壞習慣是拖延。我很愛浪費時間，一天至少要拖拖拉拉個十次！我也常常咬指甲，大約一個小時就咬一次。

3 Hi. I'm Emily. I smoke a lot, about 20 cigarettes a day. My husband says that I snore sometimes, too, but only about once a week.

嗨，我是愛蜜麗。我是個菸槍，一天大概要抽 20 根菸。我先生說我有時候也會打鼾，但是大概一週只會一次。

4 I'm Harry, and I confess: I pick my nose. Not too often, though—only when no one's looking. I like to waste time, too, but I can usually stop myself from procrastinating too much.

我是哈瑞，我坦承我會挖鼻孔，不過沒有常常挖──沒有人看到的時候我才會挖。我也很愛浪費時間，可是我通常會克制自己不要太過於拖拖拉拉。

5 Hello. I'm Tina. My bad habit is biting my nails. I bite them about three times a day. I also pick my nose on a regular basis, about once every couple of hours. My boyfriend hates it.

哈囉，我是蒂娜。我的壞習慣是咬指甲，一天要咬個三次左右。我還會固定挖鼻孔，大約幾個小時就要挖一次。我的男朋友很討厭我那樣。

IV Now, Grammar Time! p. 94

4
2 Most of my colleagues love baseball.
3 Both of my sisters can cook.
4 Some of my friends bite their nails.
5 All of my brothers snore.

5
2 Most of	3 All of	4 Most of
5 Some of	6 Both of	

V Now, Time to Speak! p. 96

6

Translation (133)

A	你有固定做什麼運動嗎？
B	有，我很愛打美式足球。
A	你多久打一次？
B	一個星期和我同學打三次左右，我是校隊隊員。
A	你打得很好嗎？
B	你開玩笑嗎？我每一場比賽都達陣得分耶。
A	哇！那真的很厲害。

7

Translation Sample Answers

Peter	Do you have any hidden talents, Sandy?
Sandy	_Yes, I can bake._
Peter	Really? I never knew that! When did you learn how to _bake_?
Sandy	I learned _when I was 13_. _My mom_ taught me.
Peter	And how often do you do it now?
Sandy	Now? _About three times a week_. I usually _bake cakes for friends_.
Peter	I see. How about party tricks? Do you have one of those?
Sandy	Well, I can _do a card trick_, but that's all. It's not very impressive. What's yours?

Peter	I can _do a backflip_ .
Sandy	_Wow, I'm impressed_ ! I wish I could do that!

彼德	珊蒂,你有什麼不為人知的才能嗎?
珊蒂	有,我會烘焙。
彼德	真的嗎?我都不知道耶!你什麼時候學烘焙?
珊蒂	我 13 歲的時候學的,我媽教我的。
彼德	那你現在多久烘焙一次?
珊蒂	現在嗎?大概一個禮拜三次,我通常烤蛋糕給朋友吃。
彼德	我了解了。派對把戲呢?你會嗎?
珊蒂	嗯,我只會變紙牌魔術而已,不是很厲害啦。你呢?
彼德	我會後空翻。
珊蒂	哇,好厲害!真希望我也會!

VI Now, Time to Pronounce!
p. 97

10　[o]　told, old, moat, bold, toad　136

　　[ɔ]　walk, fawn, crawled, yawning　137

Unit 12

I Topic Preview
p. 98　138

1
Hello. I'm calling about the apartment. Is it still available?

- -

Hello. I'm calling about the ad that was in today's paper.

- -

Hello. I saw your notice about an apartment for rent.

▸ 喂,我打電話來問公寓的事,請問還在出租嗎?

- -

喂,我看到今天報紙上的一則廣告,所以打電話來詢問。

- -

喂,我看到你們公告説有公寓要出租。

2
Where is it exactly?
It's on Newton Road, number five.
Your ad says it's a one-bedroom apartment.
Yes, that's right.
How many rooms are there altogether?
Altogether, there are four rooms.
Is it furnished?
No, it's unfurnished.

And how much is the rent?
It's $1,500 a month.
Are utilities included in the rent?
Water is included, but not electricity or gas.

▸ 請問詳細的地址在哪裡?
在牛頓路 5 號。
你們的廣告上面説是單一臥室的公寓。
對,沒錯。
一共有多少個房間?
一共有四個房間。
有附家具嗎?
沒有附家具。
租金是多少?
一個月 1500 元。
水電瓦斯費有含在租金裡嗎?
有含水費,但是不含電費和瓦斯費。

3
We should take turns cleaning the apartment.
We should keep air conditioner use to a minimum.
We should split the bills 50-50.
We should check with each other before inviting friends over.

▸ 我們應該輪流打掃房子。
我們應該把空調使用量降到最低。
我們應該平均分攤帳單。
如果要找自己的朋友來,應該先跟對方商量。

Sentence Patterns
140　p. 99

- 喂,我打電話來詢問公寓的事,請問還有要出租嗎?
- 請問詳細的地址在哪裡?/請問地址是哪裡?
- 有幾間房間?/你們廣告上説這間公寓有兩個房間。
- 有廚房嗎?/有附家具嗎?/鄰近地區是什麼樣子?/附近有地鐵站嗎?
- 租金是多少?
一個月 1,600 元。
- 有含水電費嗎?
含水費,但是不含瓦斯費和電費。
- 我們可以六四分攤租金。我們應該輪流洗廁所。

1
A Address   43   141
  Neighborhood   shops, a subway
                   station
  Rent $1,500
  Utilities   water, gas
  Rooms   living room, kitchen
  Furnished   a refrigerator
  Other   central heating,
                   communal

B Address   Road
  Neighborhood   quiet, apartment
  Rent $1,000
  Utilities   not included
  Rooms   bathroom, bedroom
  Furnished   double bed, TV
  Other   balcony, private

Script & Translation

A

Jake	Hello. I'm calling about the apartment. Is it still available?
Landlord	Yes, it's still available.
Jake	Could you tell me where it is exactly?
Landlord	On Watt Street, number 43.
Jake	I see. Is it a good neighborhood?
Landlord	Oh, yes. It's very lively, lots of shops, and there's a subway station close by.
Jake	That's convenient. How about the rent?
Landlord	It's $1,500 a month, but water and gas are included.
Jake	And could you tell me about the rooms?
Landlord	Sure. There are four rooms: a bathroom, a big bedroom, a living room, and a kitchen.
Jake	Is the apartment furnished?
Landlord	Partly. There's a refrigerator and a double bed, but no other furniture.
Jake	And how about air conditioning?
Landlord	Yes, there's air conditioning and also central heating for the winter.
Jake	Excellent. And what about laundry facilities?

Landlord	There are communal laundry facilities in the building.
杰克	喂，我打電話來詢問公寓的事，請問還有要出租嗎？
房東	有，還在出租中。
杰克	可以告訴我詳細的地址嗎？
房東	在華特街 43 號。
杰克	了解。附近的環境好不好？
房東	喔，很好。這邊挺熱鬧的，有很多商店，附近也有地鐵站。
杰克	那樣很方便，請問租金是多少？
房東	一個月 1,500 元，含水費和瓦斯費。
杰克	可以說一下房間的狀況嗎？
房東	可以，有四個房間：一間浴室、一間大臥房、一間客廳和一間廚房。
杰克	這間公寓有附家具嗎？
房東	有附一部分，有冰箱和一張雙人床，沒有其他家具。
杰克	有沒有空調？
房東	有的，有空調，冬天還有中央暖氣。
杰克	太棒了，洗衣設備呢？
房東	建築物裡面有公共的洗衣設備。

B

Jake	Hello. I'm calling about the apartment. Is it still available?
Landlord	Yes, it's still available.
Jake	Great! What's the address?
Landlord	It's 60 Hawking Road.
Jake	OK. Is the neighborhood quite lively, or . . . ?
Landlord	It's actually a very quiet area. It's mostly other apartment buildings.
Jake	I see. And your ad said the rent is $1,000 a month, right?
Landlord	That's right. It's a studio apartment, so it's a little cheaper.
Jake	A studio, so that means there are only two rooms?
Landlord	Yes. There's a bathroom, and a bedroom and living room combined.
Jake	OK, so it's quite small then.
Landlord	It's not too small actually, and it's fully furnished. There's a double bed, a closet, a desk, and a TV.
Jake	It sounds quite cozy. Are utilities included in the rent?

Landlord	No, utilities aren't included I'm afraid.
Jake	OK. Umm . . . and laundry? Are there laundry facilities in the building?
Landlord	The apartment actually has a small balcony with private laundry facilities, so it's quite convenient for you.
杰克	喂,我打電話來詢問公寓的事,請問還有要出租嗎?
房東	有,還在出租中。
杰克	太好了!請問地址在哪裡?
房東	霍金路 60 號。
杰克	好。請問鄰近地區熱鬧嗎?還是……?
房東	那一區其實滿安靜的,大部分都是公寓大樓。
杰克	我知道了。您的廣告上面說租金是一個月 1000 元,對嗎?
房東	沒錯,這間是小套房,所以比較便宜。
杰克	小套房?所以只有兩房囉?
房東	對,有一間浴室,另一間是臥室兼客廳。
杰克	喔,所以還滿小的。
房東	其實不算小,而且家具齊全。有一張雙人床、一個衣櫥、書桌和電視。
杰克	聽起來還滿舒適的。水電費有含在租金裡嗎?
房東	沒有,不含水電費,不好意思。
杰克	好,嗯……那洗衣服呢?那棟建築裡面有洗衣設備嗎?
房東	套房的小陽台就有個人的洗衣設備,所以其實還滿方便的。

2 a, c, f, g, i, j ⌒142⌒

Apartment: B

Script & Translation

Jake	So what kind of apartment should we rent?
Girlfriend	I don't mind renting a smaller place, but having a kitchen would be nice.
Jake	OK. And how about the rent?
Girlfriend	No more than $1,300 a month.
Jake	Right. What about the kind of neighborhood?
Girlfriend	I'd prefer a quiet neighborhood, though I'd like to be near a subway station.

Jake	And what about laundry and stuff?
Girlfriend	I'd prefer private laundry. I don't want to share with everyone.
Jake	OK. Does it matter if it's furnished?
Girlfriend	It definitely needs to be furnished. We don't have enough money to buy new furniture.
杰克	所以我們應該租哪一種公寓呢?
女朋友	我不介意租小一點的地方,但如果有廚房會比較好。
杰克	好,那租金呢?
女朋友	月租不要超過 1300 元。
杰克	好,那附近要什麼樣的環境?
女朋友	我比較想要附近安靜一點的,可是又想離地鐵站近一點。
杰克	洗衣設備那些呢?
女朋友	我想要私人的洗衣設備,我不喜歡跟別人共用。
杰克	好。要考慮是否有附家具嗎?
女朋友	當然要有家具啊,我們沒有那麼多錢買新家具了。

3
2 d split the rent 60-40 ⌒143⌒
3 c keep loud music to a minimum
4 b check with each other before inviting people round
5 a keep the kitchen clean

Script & Translation

1 Man	What should we do about taking out the trash? I don't want to do it every day.
Woman	OK. How about I take it out on Mondays, Wednesdays, and Fridays?
Man	That sounds fair. And I'll do it on Tuesdays, Thursdays, and Saturdays.
男	我們要怎麼分配倒垃圾的事?我不想每天倒。
女	好吧,不然星期一、三、五,我來倒垃圾?
男	那樣挺公平的,星期二、四、六換我。
2 Man	I don't think I should pay half of the rent.
Woman	Why not?
Man	Well, because your bedroom is bigger than mine, and you have your own bathroom.
Woman	Hmm, you're right. OK. How about I pay 60% of the rent?

29

男	我覺得我不應該出一半租金。	
女	為什麼？	
男	因為你的房間比我的大，而且你還有自己的浴室。	
女	嗯，也對。好吧，那我出六成的租金可以嗎？	

3	Woman	Hey, I'm trying to do some homework, but I can't concentrate.
	Man	Oh, I'm really sorry. Is it the music? Is it too loud?
	Woman	Yeah, a little. Maybe we should try not to play loud music. I think it's disturbing the neighbors, too.
	女	嘿，我要做功課，但是沒辦法專心。
	男	噢，真的很對不起，是因為音樂嗎？是不是太大聲了？
	女	對，有一點。也許我們盡量不要播太大聲的音樂，我覺得那樣也會吵到鄰居。

4	Woman	Oh! All your friends are here! I didn't know they were coming over.
	Man	Yeah, sorry. Is that a problem?
	Woman	No, of course not. But I invited my mom and dad over for dinner tonight.
	Man	Oh no! OK, in future we should check with each other before bringing friends or family round.
	女	噢，你的朋友都在啊！我不知道他們要來。
	男	對啊，對不起。這樣會打擾到你嗎？
	女	不會，當然不會。可是我今天晚上約了爸媽過來吃晚飯。
	男	噢，不！好吧，以後我們要帶朋友或家人來的話，還是先跟對方商量一下好了。

5	Woman	This kitchen is so dirty. No one has cleaned it for weeks!
	Man	Yuck, you're right. We need to do something about this.
	Woman	Yeah, I think we need to try our best to keep this place tidy. I mean, we do make food here.
	女	這個廚房好髒喔，好幾個禮拜沒人清掃了！
	男	唉喲，沒錯。我們得處理一下。
	女	對啊，我們應該盡量維持這裡的整潔，畢竟這裡是煮飯的地方。

IV Now, Grammar Time! p. 102

4
2 A few of the apartments
3 many of the problems
4 a little of the apartment
5 much of the rent

V Now, Time to Speak! p. 103

5

Translation   Sample Answers

1	Caller	Hello. I'm calling about the apartment. _Is it still available?_
	Landlord	Yes, it's still available. Would you like to come and see it?
	Caller	Maybe. _Can I ask you some questions first?_
	Landlord	Sure. Ask away.
	Caller	The ad says it's a two-bedroom apartment. _How many rooms are there altogether?_
	Landlord	There are five rooms altogether: two bedrooms, _a living room, a bathroom and a kitchen_.
	來電者	喂，我打電話來問公寓的事，還有要租嗎？
	房東	有的，還在出租中。你要來看房子嗎？
	來電者	可能會吧。我可以先問你一些問題嗎？
	房東	可以，請問。
	來電者	廣告上面說公寓有兩間臥室，那麼一共有幾房？
	房東	一共有五房：兩間臥室、一間客廳、一間浴室和一間廚房。

2	Caller	_Is the apartment furnished?_
	Landlord	_Yes, partly_. There's a refrigerator, beds, and closets, but no tables or chairs.
	Caller	_And how much is the rent?_
	Landlord	The rent is $2,500 a month.
	Caller	Are utilities included in that?
	Landlord	_Water and gas are included_, but not electricity.
	Caller	_And what's the neighborhood like?_

Landlord	It's very lively. There are lots of <u>shops and restaurants</u> nearby.
Caller	OK. Can I come round to see it this afternoon?
Landlord	Sure. Come round any time after 2:00 p.m.
來電者	<u>這間公寓有附家具嗎？</u>
房東	有附部分家具，有冰箱、床、衣櫥，但是沒有桌椅。
來電者	<u>那麼租金是多少？</u>
房東	月租是 2,500 元。
來電者	租金有包含水電嗎？
房東	有含水費和瓦斯費，不含電費。
來電者	<u>附近的環境怎麼樣？</u>
房東	很熱鬧，附近有很多<u>商店和餐廳</u>。
來電者	好，我今天下午過去看房子可以嗎？
房東	可以啊，下午兩點以後都可以來。

7

Translation Sample Answers

1 We should split the electricity bill 60-40. You use more electricity than I do, so I'll pay 40%.
我們應該六四分攤電費，你的用電量比我大，所以我應該出 40%。

2 We need to keep the living room clean. We should take turns cleaning.
我們應該保持客廳整潔，我們應該輪流打掃。

3 We should check with each other before we watch TV. Maybe we can take turns watching the TV shows we like.
我們看電視之前應該和對方商量，或許我們可以輪流看自己想看的電視節目。

4 You should go outside on the balcony to smoke.
你應該到外面陽台去抽菸。

5 You should keep the bath clean. Always wash it after you use it.
你應該保持浴缸乾淨，用過之後一定要清洗。

6 You should keep singing in the living room to a minimum when I'm in the house.
如果我在家，你應該盡量不要在客廳裡唱歌。

VI Now, Time to Pronounce!
p. 105

8 [u] you, two, bluebirds, flew (145)
[ʊ] Would, put, woods, brook

9 **1** [u] **2** [ʊ] **3** [ʊ] (146)
4 [u] **5** [u]

Script
1 grew **2** look **3** full **4** sue **5** spew

Unit 13

I Topic Preview
p. 106 (147)

1 Hello. Super Cab.
Hello. Could I order a cab from the Seaview Hotel to the train station, please?
Sure. When would you like your pickup?
Tomorrow morning at 9:00 a.m.
Can I have your last name, please?
Jones.

▸ 喂，超級計程車隊，您好。
喂，我要叫車從海景飯店到火車站。
好的，請問您何時要搭車？
明天早上九點。
請問貴姓？
瓊斯。

2 That'll be $18, please.
But the meter says $16.
There's an extra charge of two dollars after 10:00 p.m.
Here's $20. Keep the change.

▸ 一共是 18 元。
可是計費表上面寫 16 元。
因為晚上 10 點過後，要加收 2 元。
這裡是 20 元，不用找了。

3 Could I get a one-way ticket to Jamestown, please?
Sure. That'll be $2.50.

How much is a one-day pass?
A one-day pass is $8.50.
Until when is it valid?
It's valid until 4:30 a.m. tomorrow morning.

▸ 我要買一張到詹姆斯城的單程票。
好的，一共是 2.5 元。

一日券多少錢？
一日券是 8.5 元。
可以使用到什麼時候？
可以使用到明天早上四點半。

4

Which bus should I take?
Take the number 35 bus.
Where should I get off?
Get off at the third stop.
How long will the journey take?
It'll take about an hour.

▸ 我應該搭哪一班公車？
搭 35 路公車。
坐到哪裡下車？
在第三站下車。
車程要多久？
大概一個小時。

Sentence Patterns
(149) p. 107

- 我想叫車從火車站搭到皇家飯店。
- 請問您何時要搭車？
  今天下午五點。
- 一共是 13 元。
  可是計費表上面寫 10 元。
  有加成計費。
  這裡是 15 元，不用找了。
- 我要買一張到彼德思維爾的來回票。
- 月票多少錢？
- 使用期限到什麼時候？／什麼時候到期？
  使用期限到這個月的 27 號。
- 我可以在這裡買票嗎？／哪裡可以買路線圖？
- 我應該搭哪一班公車？
  搭前往新堡的公車。
  搭 432 路公車。
- 我要搭往新城的火車，要在哪裡上車？
  往新城的火車從哪一個月台發車？
  在／從第四月台。
- 我要在哪裡下車？
  我要在哪一站下車？
  在史蒂文森車站下車。
  在第四站下車。
- 車程要多久？
  大約兩個小時。

III Now, Time to Listen!
p. 108

1
(150)

Date	10/18	Pickup Time	11:00 a.m.
Customer	Mr. Peters		
From	Newtown Central train station		
To	the subway station on Fifth Street		

Super Cab	Hello. Super Cab.
Rob	Hello. I'd like to order a taxi from Newtown Central train station to the subway station on Fifth Street.
Super Cab	No problem, sir. When would you like your pickup?
Rob	Tomorrow morning at 11:00 a.m.
Super Cab	Can I have your last name, please?
Rob	Yes. Peters. P-E-T-E-R-S.
Super Cab	OK, Mr. Peters. Your cab will be at the station waiting for you.
超級車隊	喂，超級計程車隊，您好。
羅伯	喂，我想要叫車從新城中央火車站到第五街的地鐵站。
超級車隊	沒問題，先生。請問什麼時候要搭車？
羅伯	明天早上 11 點。
超級車隊	請問您貴姓？
羅伯	彼德斯，P-E-T-E-R-S。
超級車隊	好的，彼德斯先生。您的車會在車站等候您。

Fare	$ 23
Amount Paid	$ 25
Change	$ 0

(151)

Cab Driver	Here we are at the subway station. That'll be $23, please.
Rob	Here's $25.
Cab Driver	Thank you very much. Let me just get you your change.
Rob	It's OK. Keep the change.
Cab Driver	Oh, thank you very much, sir. Here's your receipt.
Rob	Thanks. Bye.
計程車司機	地鐵站到了，一共是 23 元。
羅伯	這裡是 25 元。
計程車司機	非常感謝您，我找錢給您。
羅伯	沒關係，不用找了。
計程車司機	喔，非常感謝您，先生，這是您的收據。
羅伯	謝謝，再見。

2 ① a ② c ③ b ④ c (152)

Customer	Excuse me. Could I buy a return ticket to Oldport, please?

Ticket Counter	Yes. No problem sir. That'll be $4.80, please.
Customer	Hmm . . . How much is a weekly pass?
Ticket Counter	A weekly pass is $17.10.
Customer	And when does it expire?
Ticket Counter	If you buy it today, it's valid until the 17th.
Customer	And is it only valid for this route?
Ticket Counter	Yes, it's only valid for trains between Newtown and Oldport.
Customer	OK. I'll take a weekly pass then, please.

顧客	不好意思，我要一張到舊港的來回票。
售票口	好的，沒問題，先生，一共 4.8 元。
顧客	嗯……一週券多少錢？
售票口	一週券是 17.10 元。
顧客	使用期限到什麼時候？
售票口	今天購買的話，使用期限到 17 號。
顧客	這張票只能搭這條路線嗎？
售票口	是的，只能搭乘新堡到舊港的鐵路線。
顧客	好，那我要買一張一週券。

3　❶ a　❷ a　❸ a　❹ b　❺ a　(153)

Script & Translation

❶ **Man**	Excuse me. I want to go to Richmond Park. Which stop do I get off at?
Woman	You need to get off at the next stop.
男	不好意思，我要去李奇蒙公園，要在哪一站下車？
女	你要在下一站下車。
❷ **Man**	Hi. I'm trying to get a train to Barnhill. Do you know where I can buy a ticket?
Woman	You can get one from one of the automatic ticket machines. The ticket counter is closed at the moment.
男	嗨，我想要搭乘到巴恩丘的火車，你知道要去哪裡買票嗎？
女	你可以用自動售票機買票，因為售票口現在已經關閉了。
❸ **Man**	Hello. Which platform does the train to Chicago leave from? Platform two or platform four?
Woman	It leaves from platform four. Hurry up. It leaves in two minutes!

男	哈囉，往芝加哥的火車從哪一個月台發車？第二還是第四月台？
女	從第四月台發車，你要快一點，火車再兩分鐘就開了。
❹ **Man**	Excuse me. Do you know how long the journey to London is?
Woman	I think it's about three hours to London from here.
男	不好意思，你知道到倫敦的車程要多久嗎？
女	我想從這裡到倫敦大概要三個小時。
❺ **Man**	Hi. I'm trying to get to Tainan. Do you know which train I should take?
Woman	Yes. Take the train that's going to Kaohsiung.
男	嗨，我想要去台南，你知道要搭哪一班火車嗎？
女	我知道，你要搭往高雄的火車。

IV　Now, Grammar Time!　p. 110

4
❶ can be found at the taxi stand outside
❷ can be paid for by credit card
❸ can be taken from Newtown Central Station
❹ must be used on the day you buy it
❺ can be boarded at bus stop number nine

5
❶ can be found at
❷ can, be used, between 4:30 and 7:30 p.m.
❸ can be taken from
❹ can, be bought

V　Now, Time to Speak!　p. 112

7

Translation　(154)

顧客	我要買一張到芝加哥的單程票。
售票員	好的，一共是 18.5 元。
顧客	使用期限到什麼時候？
售票員	只能在今天使用。
顧客	那幾點可以使用？
售票員	離峰車票只能在早上 9 點 30 分到下午 4 點 30 分，或者晚上 7 點 30 分以後使用。

VI Now, Time to Pronounce! p. 113

9

| [ʌ] son, funfair, mother, stuck, mud | 🎧156 |

| [ə] taken, the, zebra, surprised, the | 🎧157 |

10

1 [ʌ]	2 [ʌ]	3 [ə]	🎧158
4 [ə]	5 [ʌ]	6 [ʌ]	
7 [ʌ]	8 [ʌ]		

Unit 14

I Topic Preview p. 114 🎧159

1

What do you do for a living?
I'm a lawyer.
Which company do you work for?
I work for East Asia Law.
Is it a big company?
Yes, it's the biggest law firm in Tokyo.

▸ 你是做什麼的？
我是律師。
你在哪一間公司上班？
我在東亞律師事務所上班。
那是一間大公司嗎？
是啊，那是東京最大的法律事務所。

2

What hours do you work?
I usually work nine to five, but I sometimes work overtime.
I work shifts, so I often work weekends and nights.
What's your salary? I hope you don't mind me asking.
I earn around $40,000 a year.
I get paid $10 an hour.

▸ 你的工作時間是什麼時候？
我通常從九點工作到五點，有時候會加班。
我是排班的，所以週末和晚上也常常要上班。
你的薪水是多少？希望你不介意我問這個。
我的年薪大約是 40,000 元。
我的時薪是 10 元。

3

So, what do you like about your job?
I get a lot of paid vacation days, which is good.
Is there anything you hate about your job?

Yes, I hate my boss. He's the worst thing about my job.

▸ 那麼，你喜歡你的工作的哪一部分？
我的年假很多，這點很棒。
你的工作有沒有讓你討厭的地方？
有，我討厭我老闆，他是我的工作最大的缺點。

4

Why did you leave your old job?
I got fired for turning up late too often.
I wanted to try something different.

▸ 你為什麼會離開上一份工作？
我因為太常遲到被解雇。
我想嘗試一些不一樣的工作。

Sentence Patterns 🎧161 p. 115

• 你是做什麼的？
我是編輯。

• 你在哪一間公司上班？
我在牛津劍橋大學出版社上班。

• 你在哪裡工作？
我在便利商店工作。

• 你的上班時間為何？
我是固定時間上下班。／我是排班的。／
我是兼職。

• 你的薪水是多少？
我的年薪大約 35,000 元。
我只領最低工資。

• 你最喜歡工作的哪一部分？
我有很多不扣薪的事假。／我的聖誕節獎金很多。

• 你有討厭工作的哪部分嗎？
我工作最討厭的地方就是要加班。

• 你為什麼辭去上一份工作？
我辭職是為了爭取更高的薪水。

III Now, Time to Listen! p. 116

1

| 1 c | 2 f | 3 b | 4 d | 🎧162 |

1 regular office, salary, 40,000, year, sick, personal 🎧163
2 work, coffee shop, shift, by the hour
3 night, minimum wage, part-time job
4 best, vacation, paid, early at 4:00 p.m.

🎧 Translation

1 吉米・庫伯　我在首都銀行工作，我是固定時間上下班，我的薪水不錯，年薪有 40,000 元。還有很多不扣薪的病假和事假，是個不錯的工作。

2　艾瑪‧卡爾　我每個星期一、三、五在咖啡館工作，我是上早上七點半到下午三點半的班，以時薪來算工資。我有幾天不扣薪的病假，以這種工作來說，還挺不錯的。

3　艾倫‧李　我在 7-11 上晚班，領的是最低工資，只有週末上班，算是半工半讀。

4　喬西‧伯克　我的工作最好的地方就是年假！我每年都有好多不扣薪的年假。我的薪水也很優渥——年薪大約 40,000 元。而且我早早在下午四點就可以下班。

2　1 a　2 b　3 c　4 c　(164)
　　5 a　6 d

Julia | The last job I did was working in a bar. It was shift work, and I hated the hours. So, I'd like to find a job with regular office hours, maybe working in a big company or a firm. And I want to work full-time, too. My last job was part-time, and I got paid by the hour. I left because the salary was just too low. I want to earn at least $30,000 a year from now on. I'd also really like to find a job where I can work as part of a big group. The thing I liked the most about my last job was that I had lots of really great colleagues.

茱莉亞 | 我的上一份工作是在酒吧上班，是排班制，我的工作時段糟透了。所以，我想要找一份固定上下班的工作，可能到大公司或事務所工作吧。而且，我也想做全職的工作，我的上一份工作是兼職，依時薪計算，我會離職就是因為薪水實在太低了，我希望從現在起，每年至少可以賺 30,000 元。我也好希望找一份可以團隊合作的工作，我的上一份工作最讓我喜歡的地方，就是我有好多優秀的同事。

IV Now, Grammar Time!　p. 118

3　2 Peter works shifts, doesn't he?
　　3 Mark's a teacher, isn't he?
　　4 Mike earns $20,000 a year, doesn't he?
　　5 Peter gets paid sick days, doesn't he?

4　1 e　2 b　3 a　4 d　5 c

VI Now, Time to Pronounce!　p. 121

8　[ɝ]　heard, church, first, work　(166)
　　[ɚ]　farmer, number, dollars

9　1 [ɚ]　2 [ɝ]　3 [ɝ]　(167)
　　4 [ɚ]　5 [ɝ]

Script
1 over　2 search　3 third　4 bigger　5 learn

Unit 15

I Topic Preview　p. 122　(168)

1 | We went to Italy for a month.
　| Where did you go in Italy?
　| We went all over. We visited Rome, Florence, Milan, and Turin.

▶ 我們去了義大利一個月。
　你們去了義大利的哪些地方？
　我們到處走，去了羅馬、佛羅倫斯、米蘭和杜林。

2 | Tell me about Rome. What did you do there?
　| We ate some great local food, and we visited the Colosseum.

▶ 告訴我一些羅馬的事，你們在那邊做了些什麼？
　我們吃了很好吃的當地美食，還參觀了羅馬競技場。

3 | Did you meet any interesting people?
　| We met a group of other travelers from Australia and an interesting local named Giovanni.

▶ 你們有沒有遇到什麼有趣的人？
　我們遇到一團澳洲來的觀光客，還有一位很有趣的當地人，叫作喬凡尼。

4 | Did you stay in hostels the whole time?
　| Most of the time, but in Turin we stayed in a little guesthouse.
　| What were the hostels like?
　| They were fairly basic, but they were really fun places to stay.

▶ 你們全程都住在青年旅社嗎？
　幾乎都是，不過我們在杜林是住一間小民宿。

青年旅社是什麼樣子？
很陽春，不過也是很不錯的住宿地點。

5 What did you think of Italy?
The people were so passionate and friendly.
And the food?
The food was full of local flavor.
And the cities themselves?
Really spectacular. The architecture there was so striking.

▸ 你覺得義大利怎麼樣？
那裡的人好熱情又友善。
食物呢？
食物充滿了當地風味。
城市呢？
非常壯觀，那裡的建築實在是美侖美奐。

Sentence Patterns

🎧170 p. 123

- 你們去了哪裡？
  我們去法國三個禮拜。
- 去了法國的哪些地方？
  我們四處走。／我們去了法國南部。
- 你們在那裡做了些什麼？
  我們暢遊都市，還去參加了當地的慶典活動。
- 你們有沒有遇到什麼有趣的人？
  有，我們遇到一個很酷的人，叫作羅德里格。
- 你們住在哪裡？
  我們住在五星級飯店。／我們睡在臥舖車上。
- 民宿是什麼樣子？
  很基本，不過很乾淨，有家的感覺。
- 你覺得西班牙怎麼樣？
  那裡的人真是享樂主義！食物很新鮮。
  風景／建築物令人嘆為觀止。

III Now, Time to Listen!

p. 124

1 **A** **1** a **2** c   🎧171
   B **3** c **4** b

Script & Translation

A
Nicholas	Hi, Mom!
Mom	Nicholas! I'm so happy to hear your voice! Are you OK?
Nicholas	Yeah, I'm having a great time!
Mom	It's so good to hear that. So, tell me about your trip so far.
Nicholas	Well, on Monday we went on a guided tour of Paris. We visited the Eiffel Tower, the Moulin Rouge, the Arc de Triomphe—all the major sights. Then on Tuesday we visited the Palace of Versailles.
Mom	Wow! I hear Versailles is just spectacular.
Nicholas	It is, Mom. It has some of the most beautiful architecture. And the rooms inside are so luxurious.

尼可拉斯	嗨，媽！
媽	尼可拉斯！我好高興聽到你的聲音！你好嗎？
尼可拉斯	很好，我玩得很開心！
媽	那真是太好了。說些你旅行到現在的事給我聽。
尼可拉斯	嗯，星期一我們參加了巴黎導覽旅遊團，參觀了艾菲爾鐵塔、紅磨坊和凱旋門——主要觀光景點都去過了。星期二我們參觀凡爾賽宮。
媽	哇！聽說凡爾賽宮很壯觀。
尼可拉斯	的確是，媽。那裡有一些建築美得無與倫比，裡面的房間好豪華啊。

B
Mom	Have you tried any good French food, or have you only been eating at McDonald's?
Nicholas	Are you kidding? Yesterday we went to an amazing little café on the Champs-Élysées. We tried some gorgeous French cheeses, some French wine, and we had three different kinds of desserts.

媽	你有沒有吃到什麼好吃的法國料理，還是只吃麥當勞？
尼可拉斯	別開玩笑了！我們昨天去了香榭大道上一家很棒的小咖啡館，品嚐美味的法國起司，也喝了一些法國葡萄酒，我們一共吃了三種不同的點心。

2 **1** c **2** e **3** d **4** b **5** a 🎧172

1 Spain, few weeks, local festival 🎧173
2 volunteered, farm, family
3 famous sights, took, photos
4 Japan, people, wore, clothes
5 foot, shopping, ate, restaurants

Script & Translation

1 Woman
Last year I went to Spain for a few weeks. I went to a local festival called La Tomatina. It was crazy. There was a huge food fight. Everyone was throwing tomatoes at each other!

女
去年，我去西班牙玩了幾個禮拜。我參加了當地的番茄節，太瘋狂了，是一場丟食物大戰，每個人都朝著別人丟番茄！

2 Man
I volunteered on a farm in France last year. I picked grapes and helped make wine. It was hard work, but it was so nice to live with the family and eat homemade French food.

男
去年，我到法國的一個農場去體驗當志工，我去摘葡萄，幫忙釀葡萄酒。雖然很辛苦，但是和農場一家人生活、吃家常的法國菜，真的很開心。

3 Woman
I went to Brazil last month. I saw Christ the Redeemer on the mountain. It's one of the most famous sights in the world and it was unbelievable. I took about a million photos.

女
我上個月去巴西，看了山上的救世基督像，那是全世界最著名的景點之一，真的非常不可思議。我拍了一大堆照片。

4 Man
I traveled in Japan last year. The best thing about the trip was the people I met. I visited the Harajuku district a lot and met all kinds of people who wore these weird, cool clothes.

男
去年我去日本旅遊，旅途中印象最深的就是我所遇到的人。我去了原宿區好幾趟，看到各種奇裝異服的人。

5 Woman
I went to Seoul in Korea for a week last month. I just spent my time exploring the city, shopping, and eating in local restaurants. I think exploring somewhere on foot is the best way to learn about the place.

女
上個月，我去韓國首爾一個星期，所有的時間都花在走訪市內各地、購物，還有在當地的餐廳用餐。我覺得要了解一個地方，最好的方式就是走路參觀。

③
1 b **2** a, a, b **3** b, a (174)
4 b **5** a **6** b

Script & Translation

Jane
I just got home after two weeks in Japan. I stayed in Tokyo for a week and then traveled around Japan for the second week.
On my first day in Tokyo, I went on a guided tour of the city and saw sights like the Tokyo Tower and the Imperial Palace. But after that I decided to explore the city by myself. I spent lots of time checking out the shops, trying delicious, fresh sushi, and going to karaoke bars with some locals I met.
On the second half of the trip, I spent my time exploring lots of other cities around Japan by train. I spent a day in one place and then slept in a sleeper car until I arrived at the next place. I actually visited a total of six cities in only two weeks. It was great to see so much of Japan in such a short time.

珍
我才剛從日本結束兩週的行程回到家。我在東京待了一週，第二週則在日本四處旅行。
在東京的第一天，我參加了市區導覽團，造訪了東京鐵塔和皇居這些景點。後來我還是決定自己到市區探索一番。我花了很多時間逛商店、品嚐新鮮美味的壽司，還和我遇到的一些當地人一起去卡拉OK吧。
這次旅行的後半段，我搭火車造訪了日本各地其他都市。我會在一個地方待個一天，然後睡臥舖車到下一個地點。短短兩個星期內，我就去了六個都市。可以在這麼短的時間內，好好地認識日本，真是一件很棒的事。

IV Now, Grammar Time!
p. 127

④
1 to take **2** to eat **3** partying
4 eating **5** to book

⑤
1 a **2** b **3** b **4** a **5** b (175)

Script & Translation

1 **Woman** | I remember visiting the Eiffel Tower in Paris.
女 | 我記得在巴黎時參觀了艾菲爾鐵塔。

2 **Man** | I tried singing karaoke in Tokyo, but it wasn't for me.
男 | 我在東京嘗試了唱卡拉 OK，但我還是不愛。

3 **Woman** | I tried to explore the city by myself, but I got lost too often.
女 | 我嘗試自己走訪都市各角落，但是常常迷路。

4 **Man** | I stopped to ask for directions.
男 | 我停下來問路。

5 **Woman** | I must remember to write you a postcard.
女 | 我一定要記得寫明信片給你。

V Now, Time to Speak! p. 128

7

Translation Sample Answers

A I went to Tokyo for a week.
B Wow! That sounds great. Tell me about it.
A I saw/visited the Tokyo Tower and the Imperial Palace.
B That sounds amazing. What else did you do?
A I ate some great local food, like sushi and sashimi. They were so tasty.
B Did you do any fun activities?
A Oh, yeah. One day I climbed Mount Fuji!
B That sounds so exciting! Did you go to any festivals or parties?
A Yeah, I went to a karaoke bar. It was so much fun. I sang lots of old songs there. Oh! And I met a crazy girl named Azami there, too.
B Ha! He/She/They sound(s) like a lot of fun. So, what did you think of Tokyo overall?
A I thought the food was/were fresh and delicious, the people was/were polite but lots of fun, and the architecture was/were really impressive.

A 我去東京一個禮拜。
B 哇！好棒，快跟我說。
A 我去看／參觀了東京鐵塔和皇居。
B 聽起來好棒喔，你還做了些什麼？
A 我吃了當地美食，像是壽司和生魚片，好好吃。
B 你有做些什麼好玩的活動嗎？
A 喔，有。有一天我去爬富士山！
B 好刺激喔！你有沒有參加慶典或派對？
A 有啊，我去卡拉 OK 吧，好好玩，我在那裡唱好多首老歌。喔！我在那裡還認識了一個很瘋狂的女孩子，她叫淺見。
B 哈！他／她／他們聽起來好像很有趣。那麼，你對東京的整體印象怎麼樣？
A 我覺得食物很新鮮又美味，那裡的人既有禮又有趣，建築物也讓人印象深刻。

VI Now, Time to Pronounce! p. 131

9 1 tile 2 lighter 3 boil 4 sigh 5 hoist (177)

10 1 bow 2 mouse 3 trice (179)

11 (180)
[aɪ] bright, sky, smiled
[ɔɪ] boys, boiled, koi
[aʊ] tower, dour, our

Unit 16

I Topic Preview p. 132 (181)

1
Is this the check-in desk for flight KL 878?
Yes. May I see your passport, please?
Do you need to see my e-ticket?
Yes, I need to see your booking number.

How many bags will you be checking in?
Just this suitcase, but I also have one carry-on bag.
Could you put your suitcase on the scale, please?

▸ 請問這裡是 KL 878 班機的報到櫃檯嗎？
是的，請給我您的護照好嗎？
你需要看我的電子機票嗎？
是的，我需要看您的訂位編號。

請問您要託運幾件行李？
只有這旅行箱，但我有一個包包要當客艙行李。
請把您的旅行箱放在磅秤上。

2
Would it be possible to get a window seat?
Let me just check. Yes, there are window seats available. Here's your boarding pass and baggage claim tag.

Thank you. What time does the flight board?
Your flight boards at 9:30 p.m. from Gate D6.

▸ 可以給我靠窗的座位嗎？
我查查看。可以的，還有靠窗的座位。這是您的登機證和行李提領證。
謝謝。請問幾點可以登機？
您的班機將在晚間 9 點 30 分，於 D6 登機門登機。

③ Passengers with seat numbers 68 to 51 may now start boarding the plane.
This is the final call for passenger David Chang traveling on flight AA 1476. Please proceed immediately to Gate G7 for boarding.
Flight KL 678 to Bangkok will be delayed due to poor weather conditions. More information will be given shortly.

▸ 座位號碼 68 到 51 的乘客，現在可以開始登機。
這是 AA 1476 班機最後一次的登機廣播，請乘客張大衛先生立即前往 G7 登機門登機。
飛往曼谷的 KL 678 班機，因天候不佳，將延遲抵達，我們稍後將為您提供更多資訊。

④ What's the purpose of your visit?
Tourism.
How long do you plan to stay?
Two weeks.
Where are you staying?
The Holiday Inn in Oxford.
Do you have a return ticket?
Yes. Here it is.

▸ 請問您此行的目的是什麼？
觀光。
您預計停留多久？
兩週。
您的住宿地點是？
牛津的假日酒店。
您有回程機票嗎？
有，在這裡。

Sentence Patterns 🎧183 p. 133

- 請問這裡是 KL 878 班機的報到櫃檯嗎？
- 你需要看我的機票嗎？
- 我要託運這個旅行箱。
- 我還有一個包包要當客艙行李。
  這個包包可以當客艙行李嗎？
- 可以給我靠窗的座位嗎？

- 登機時間是什麼時候？
  您的班機是晚上 7 點 45 分開始登機。
- 我要在哪一個登機門登機？
  您要在 F5 登機門登機。
- 請問您此行的目的是？
  觀光。／洽公。／探親。
- 您計畫在這裡停留多久？
  三週。
- 您的住宿地點是？
  伯明罕的皇家飯店。
- 您有回程機票嗎？
  有，在這裡。

Ⅲ Now, Time to Listen! p. 134

① ❶ a   ❷ b   ❸ a   🎧184

ⓐ 22:30   ⓑ BA 578   ⓒ D8   🎧185
ⓓ 31C   ⓔ Paris

Script & Translation

Paul	Hello. Is this the check-in desk for flight BA 578 to Paris?
Staff	Yes, sir. May I see your passport, please?
Paul	Of course. Do you need to see my e-ticket?
Staff	No, that won't be necessary. Just your passport is fine.
Paul	Here you are.
Staff	OK. Thank you. Would you like a window seat or an aisle seat?
Paul	Can I have an aisle seat, please?
Staff	Of course. Seat 31C. And do you have any luggage to check in?
Paul	Yes, my suitcase. I have this other bag, too. Is it okay as a carry-on?
Staff	Yes, that should be fine. Could you put your suitcase on the scale, please?
Paul	OK.
Staff	Twenty kilograms. That's no problem. Here's your boarding pass and baggage claim tag. Your flight boards at 22:30, and the boarding gate is Gate D8.
Paul	Thank you very much.
保羅	哈囉，請問這裡是飛往巴黎的班機 BA 578 的報到櫃檯嗎？
職員	是的，先生。麻煩給我您的護照好嗎？
保羅	好的，你需要看我的電子機票嗎？

職員	不用，只要您的護照就可以了。
保羅	給你。
職員	好的，謝謝您。請問您要靠窗還是靠走道的座位？
保羅	可以給我靠走道的嗎？
職員	沒問題，座位號碼 31C。您有行李要託運嗎？
保羅	有，我的旅行箱。我還有這個包包，可以隨身攜上飛機嗎？
職員	可以的，這個沒問題。請把您的旅行箱放在磅秤上好嗎？
保羅	好。
職員	20 公斤，沒超重。這是您的登機證和行李提領證。您的登機時間是 22 點 30 分，登機門是 D8。
保羅	非常感謝你。

2   1 a, c, d   2 c, d   3 b, c   🎧186

1 final, passenger / SQ 1476 / boarding / takeoff   🎧187
2 small children / requiring / assistance / pass / passport
3 flight / delayed / time / departure / Gate B6

🎧 Translation

1 請注意，這是新加坡航空公司飛往倫敦 SQ 1476 班機最後一次的登機廣播，請乘客亨利・李先生即刻前往 F5 登機門登機。本班機已準備起飛，這是最後一次登機廣播，請乘客亨利・李即刻登機。

2 請注意，美國航空公司飛往芝加哥的 AA 249 班機可以開始登機，身邊有孩童或需要特殊協助的乘客，請開始登機。請備妥您的登機證與護照，以供查驗。

3 搭乘中華航空公司飛往北京的 CI 547 班機乘客請注意，本班機因飛機細微技術問題，將延遲起飛。本班機目前的登機時間為 15 點 35 分，登機門也變更至 B6。本公司為造成您的不便深表歉意。

IV Now, Grammar Time!
p. 136

3
1 The water bottle is so big that it can't fit in the transparent bag.
2 This passport is so old that you can't use it.
3 This knife is so dangerous that you can't take it on the plane.
4 First-class tickets are so expensive that I can't afford them.

4
1 too late to get a window seat
2 too sharp to take in your carry-on bag
3 too windy to take off
4 too early to check in

V Now, Time to Speak!
p. 137

5
🎧 Translation   🎧188

旅客	哈囉，請問這裡是飛往多倫多 SQ 578 班機的報到櫃檯嗎？
櫃檯人員	是的，先生。您的護照麻煩一下。
旅客	好的，你要看我的電子機票嗎？
櫃檯人員	不需要，您的護照就可以了。
旅客	給你。
櫃檯人員	好的，謝謝您。請問您要靠窗還是靠走道的座位？
旅客	請給我靠窗的座位。
櫃檯人員	好的，您的座位是 23A。請問您有行李要託運嗎？
旅客	有，一個旅行箱。我還有一個筆電包，可以隨身攜上飛機嗎
櫃檯人員	可以，沒有問題的。麻煩您把旅行箱放在磅秤上好嗎？
旅客	好。
櫃檯人員	不好意思，這個旅行箱超重兩公斤，需要付行李超重費 50 元。
旅客	噢，天啊。好吧，我用信用卡支付。
櫃檯人員	都辦理好了，先生。這是您的登機證和行李提領證，您的班機登機時間是 22 點 30 分，登機門是 D8。
旅客	非常謝謝你。

VI Now, Time to Pronounce!
p. 139

10
🎧 Translation   🎧192

A	不好意思，請問這裡是 KL 945 班機的報到櫃檯嗎？
B	是的，請給我您的護照。
A	你也需要看我的電子機票嗎？
B	不需要。好的，請問您要什麼座位？
A	我要靠窗的座位。
B	沒問題。
A	噢，我想確認一下，這個包包可以隨身攜上飛機吧？
B	可以的。好了，您的班機將於 7 點 30 分開始登機，您的登機門是 E6。
A	謝謝。